ALONE TOGETHER

"There." Hannah pointed toward the supporting beam across from her. "Something's shining in the passing candlelight."

David leaned carefully over the space between them and the wall. He handed Hannah the candle and then braced one hand on the beam while he reached behind it with the other. Hannah held her breath as he drew a small gold statue into the light.

"Well done, Miss Alexander," David murmured. "I've already passed that spot twice and never saw this. You've earned your keep this day."

Hannah felt warmly pleased by his praise. She glanced up at him and saw that he was once more smiling at her over the candle. As their gazes met, the smile slowly faded, to be replaced by an intensity in his sapphire eyes that made her catch her breath once more.

"Such hard work deserves a reward," he murmured, leaning toward her. Hannah swallowed, sure that she must have mistaken him. But he bent his head and pressed his lips to hers.

She closed her eyes as the sweetest of sensations rippled through her. His lips were warm and gentle. They brushed against hers with the softness of silk. Her knees were shaking.

David had been wrong, Hannah thought. The house's secret passages were dangerous, perhaps as dangerous as the singing of her heart.

Books by Regina Scott

THE UNFLAPPABLE MISS FAIRCHILD
THE TWELVE DAYS OF CHRISTMAS
"SWEETER THAN CANDY" IN
A MATCH FOR MOTHER
THE BLUESTOCKING ON HIS KNEE
CATCH OF THE SEASON
"A PLACE BY THE FIRE" IN MISTLETOE KITTENS

Published by Zebra Books

A
DANGEROUS
DALLIANCE

Regina Scott

Zebra Books
Kensington Publishing Corp.
http://www.zebrabooks.com

ZEBRA BOOKS are published by

Kensington Publishing Corp.
850 Third Avenue
New York, NY 10022

First Printing: May, 2000
10 9 8 7 6 5 4 3 2 1

Printed in the United States of America

To my dear friend and sister in all but blood,
Nancy Robak,
in hopes that she will one day find her David.

One

To Hannah Alexander, people existed to be painted. Every wise old crone with a youthful twinkle in her eye, every stout gentleman of military bearing, every wide-eyed child with an endearing smile was a moment to be captured, re-created, embellished until the essence of them shone from her canvas for all to see. When she looked at those around her, she saw them frozen in a moment of perfection that illuminated their souls. The farmer carrying a lamb home on his shoulders at sunset was the Good Shepherd. The girl flirting with the farmer's son outside church on Sunday was Aphrodite Taunting Hephaestus. The other teachers at the Barnsley School for Young Ladies gossiping about their charges' parents were the Three Witches from *Macbeth*. She thought she would be completely happy if only she could spend her days with her paint box and easel. And now, after years of dreaming, it looked as if she might actually attain that happiness.

She smiled as she gazed across her crowded classroom. Overall, the Barnsley School had not been a bad place to work the last three years since she had left home. She had been able to convince Miss Martingale, the headmistress, to let her use this first-floor room facing the south, so that her students might have good light for their lessons. Spring sunlight streamed through the wide windows and lit the room with a warm glow. Today it was oil painting, one of her favorite subjects. A dozen fifteen-, sixteen-, and seventeen-year-old young ladies, in sprigged muslin as bright as the jonquils outside the window, frowned at the canvases on their easels. Their painting smocks barely concealed their blossoming charms. The Muses Hard at Work, her artist's mind declared. For at least half of them, this would be their final project. Within the next few weeks, they would graduate and head off to London for the Season. With any luck, Hannah would be joining them, but as a professional artist, not a marriageable miss.

She allowed a sigh of anticipation to escape her. Was it truly possible that she was going to London to become a portrait painter? She could hardly believe her good fortune. Just three months ago, the Earl of Prestwick had inquired whether the school's art teacher would be willing to attempt a portrait of the dowager countess. It was well-known about Barnsley and the surrounding villages that Lady Prestwick was a gentle, retiring soul, easily frightened by the world around her. She was seldom seen outside the gates of her fine estate. Hannah had been more than willing to paint the beautiful countess, who put her in mind of Elaine in the legends of King Arthur. Elaine had pined away for her love of Lancelot, and it seemed to Hannah Lady Prestwick's sad smiles mirrored a similar melancholy. The resulting painting had been heralded by the earl and the local gentry alike as a fine work of art.

Since then, Squire Pentercast's lovely wife had requested that Hannah undertake a painting of their family. In addition, one of the more influential of the parents, the Duke of Emerson, had suggested that she paint him upon his return from Vienna. As the squire's wife was well-known in social circles, and the duke was a famous diplomat, Hannah was assured of at least the beginning of a promising career. It was more than she had ever hoped for. She planned to finish her painting of the Pentercasts by Easter and put in her notice to Miss Martingale shortly thereafter. With the money from her two commissions and what she had saved working at the school for the last three years, she had enough to live on frugally in London for a year, while she built her reputation and her clientele. For the first time in her life, her dreams were within her grasp.

Her attention was drawn to a whispered debate that was rising steadily in volume. Three of her students were clustered around the easel of a fourth, and by the animated gestures and giggles, the topic did not appear to be brush strokes. Hannah frowned at them, but as usual, they paid her no heed. She cleared her throat, and several of the younger girls looked up. The four in question only became more excited. Hannah squared her shoulders.

Playing the disciplinarian was one part of her job she was not going to miss. She was aware that often she held control of the room by the slimmest of threads. She had never mastered the technique of intimidating her students with her authority that so many of the other teachers used. In truth, she suspected that most of her older students knew she was only twenty-two, barely five years older than they were. They had only to look at her five feet, four inches to see she did not tower over any of them. To make matters worse, she was cursed with a clear-skinned, oval face and large doelike eyes that seemed to encourage condescending smiles rather than strict obedience. She did have a small mole in the lash line of her left eye, but it was a warm brown and smooth, with nary a hair to make it formidable. Her own nose was short and pert, and her mouth tended far too often to smile. No, she had not been the most awe-inspiring of teachers, although her students did seem to learn their lessons and more than one parent had complimented her on the girls' knowledge of art.

Still, she could not allow the current debate to disrupt

her class. Hannah moved quietly across the room until she was standing directly behind her students. Unfortunately, even that failed to deter them.

"I tell you, it will be a week to end all weeks," declared Priscilla Tate. That Priscilla was the center of attention did not surprise Hannah. With the girl's warm blond hair and emerald eyes, she was by far the loveliest of the graduating class. She was also one of the least popular, for all her considerable family connections. Priscilla had a way of flaunting her beauty and accomplishments at her classmates. Hannah had long ago begun to think of her as Hera Among the Lesser Goddesses. Today did not seem to be the exception.

"And you can bring all three of us? Your aunt is beyond generous!" This from Daphne Courdebas, the most athletic of the graduates. Everything about Daphne was long and lean, from her limbs to her light brown hair. And all of it had a tendency to tangle unmercifully in her unbridled enthusiasm for life. Amazon in Training, Hannah thought.

"And her still in mourning! How kind!" Ariadne Courdebas put in. At a year younger than her sister, Ariadne could easily have been from another family entirely. She was round and baby-faced, with lank brown hair, great vapid blue eyes, and a morbid fascination with illness. Not a week passed that Hannah was not taking the girl to the nurse over some imagined disease. It was amazing how truly distressed that round face could look, like Lot's Wife Looking Back at Sodom.

"She's no doubt overcome with sorrow from the loss of her husband and stepson," put in Lady Emily Southwell. The Priestess of Delphi, Hannah thought, her artist's mind painting the picture. Lady Emily would have made such a marvelous seer. Her deep-set brown eyes, black frizzy hair, sallow complexion, and pinched nose were perfectly matched to her dismal view of the world. She even wore the dark colors and austere tailoring, like the brown silk gown that was nearly as depressing as Hannah's stiff black bombazine uniform. Nonetheless, Lady Emily was one of Hannah's favorite students, for she was the only student who had shown the least promise as an artist at the Barnsley School for Young Ladies. Hannah was sure that it was her own recognition of Lady Emily's promise, as well as Hannah's talent, that had resulted in Lady Emily's father, the Duke of Emerson, suggesting that Hannah paint him as well.

"Girls," Hannah said firmly. "That is enough. Return to your lessons."

Daphne jumped, and Ariadne looked abashed. Lady Emily turned willingly to her painting, a dark rendition of the crucifixion. Priscilla rolled her emerald eyes and pouted.

"You don't understand, Miss Alexander. My aunt, Lady Brentfield, has invited us to stay with her until Easter. We have a number of important preparations to make."

Hannah hid a smile at the girl's imperious tone. "No doubt you do. And no doubt they can wait until class is dismissed. Return to your easel, Miss Tate."

"Oh, honestly," Priscilla snapped, flouncing back to her place. The ruffles on the hem of her sprigged muslin gown danced about her legs. Even annoyed and annoying, the girl managed to look graceful. Hannah shook her head and watched until Ariadne and Daphne returned to their places as well.

She had hoped that would be the end of the matter, but they remained in their places only for a few moments, and then Daphne skirted back to Priscilla's easel to begin frantic whispering again. Hannah disliked raising her voice to her students, so she strode back to their side once more, this time with far less charity.

"I tell you we cannot go without a chaperone," Daphne was maintaining heatedly as she approached.

"It's only a day's drive to the estate," Priscilla replied,

tossing her golden curls. "Surely your mother would allow you to go that far."

"My mother wouldn't allow me to go as far as the dining room without a chaperone," Daphne argued with a martyred sigh. "Can't your aunt send someone?"

"I'm not going to ask her for favors after she agreed to let the whole lot of you come with me," Priscilla chided. "Besides, she sent a letter of instruction to Miss Martingale. Perhaps she asked for a chaperone."

"Girls," Hannah warned, stepping forcefully between them.

Priscilla muttered something that did not sound the least like an apology and steadfastly returned her gaze to the few blobs of paint she had managed to affix to her canvas.

Daphne started to turn away, then whirled back so quickly she almost upset Priscilla's easel. "I have it!" she cried as Hannah caught the veering canvas. "Miss Alexander can be our chaperone!"

A lead brick seemed to crash from Hannah's throat to her stomach. Her, a chaperone? Mixing with the aristocracy in social matters far beyond her ken? Delaying her own plans by weeks? It was unthinkable. "That is enough, Miss Courdebas," she managed, finding it difficult to breathe at the very thought. "I am not a chaperone. Return to your work or I will set you to cleaning paint pots during your free time."

Daphne, who was known to prefer riding during her free time, blanched and hurried back to her spot. For once, the stern look on Hannah's face was enough to deter further conversation for the rest of the class period.

She managed to put the distressing incident out of her mind until she was called to the headmistress's office later that afternoon. She went expecting some information on her role in the upcoming graduation ceremony. In the past, she had had the ignoble job of painting signs to show the parents the direction of the retiring rooms. This year her one friend at the school, the literature teacher Eleanor Pritchett, was in charge of the event, and Hannah had hopes of a more meaningful role. Miss Martingale had other thoughts on her mind.

"Priscilla Tate's aunt, Lady Brentfield, has graciously invited some of the girls for Easter holiday," she proclaimed without preamble. "I need you as chaperone."

Hannah felt herself pale, but forced her dutiful smile to remain in place. She had always been able to reasonably discuss things with her employer. Surely Miss Martingale would not send her off simply to gratify the whims of four students. "But I know nothing about deportment, Miss Martingale," she pointed out. "As you know, I was raised quietly in the country."

The large, dark-haired woman shrugged. "That is not important. Lady Brentfield can be counted on to enforce the social niceties. I need someone to chaperone them in the carriage on the ride to and from the estate, and Lady Brentfield has requested that we provide someone to assist her in monitoring the girls' activities when she is unavailable. So busy a woman as Lady Brentfield cannot be expected to watch them every minute. She has an estate to manage."

So, Hannah was just supposed to be a faceless servant, at the beck and call of the socially astute Lady Brentfield. If the assignment had had any appeal before, it had none now. Hannah had only met Lady Brentfield a few times when the lady had visited the school, usually when she was fetching Priscilla or returning her from some event. But Hannah knew that her ladyship was a powerful influence. Miss Martingale gloated over Lady Brentfield's least kindness, and many of the teachers watched from the upper windows of the school to catch a glimpse of the latest styles the woman wore. Hannah could not imagine anything more mortifying than having to flutter about in the wake of this fashionable woman, her own lack of polish and ignorance of the upper class showing with each movement. "Lady Brentfield will surely want someone with whom the girls are comfortable," she protested. "I barely know them."

"That is as it should be. You know my policy that students and teachers should not fraternize. I have observed that you keep a distance from your students, which I applaud. I have also observed that they tend to ignore your commands. This trip will give you an opportunity to practice your discipline skills."

Practicing her discipline skills was the last thing on Hannah's mind, as was spending a week in close company with her students. The distance Miss Martingale had noted was there for a reason. She was trying to hide the fact that her students scared her not a little. Her fear was easy to hide when she could focus on art, but she was sure they'd see right through her if she was forced to interact with them socially. Besides, spending a week at the Brentfield estate would delay her commission.

"But I've just agreed to paint Squire Pentercast and his family," she explained to Miss Martingale, hoping the mention of the local landowner would inspire sufficient respect to allow her to remain. "I'm sure one of the other teachers would love to go."

"Most have arranged to go home to their families," Miss Martingale replied, her considerable bulk beginning to tremble in indignation that Hannah continued to question her judgment. "And I cannot spare Miss Pritchett; she is needed to finish the preparations for the graduation ceremony. Besides, Lady Brentfield was most emphatic about the type of teacher she wanted: quiet, unassuming, dutiful. I am certain you fit that description."

Nearly every teacher at the Barnsley School fit that description, but Hannah could see by the steel in Miss Martingale's eyes that further argument was useless. She considered for a moment tendering her resignation right that moment, but she needed her final two weeks of salary and all of her commission money if she was to have enough to live in London.

That night after the girls were in bed, she poured out her frustrations to Eleanor, who with her long elegant body and light brown hair would have been so much more suitable as the chaperone. Hannah had always thought Eleanor should be painted as Joan of Arc or perhaps the goddess Athena. She was certainly clever and capable enough to manage some great feat far more challenging than serving as the literature teacher at the Barnsley School.

"I've had my fill of great houses," Eleanor had assured her when she had confided her problem. "As I told you, I spent a summer with the Earl and Countess of Wenworth tutoring their son, and that was quite enough for me. I'm sorry to say that I agree with Miss Martingale, but there is an undefinable line between the aristocracy and those of us who work for a living, Hannah. When we cross that line, everyone suffers."

Hannah frowned. "Is the gulf between us so wide? My grandfather always said that all men are equal before God."

Eleanor smiled. "Your grandfather was a minister, if memory serves. He was supposed to think well of everyone. And you are just like him. I promise you, there is a tremendous gulf. It is one thing to teach the appreciation and application of art to the daughters of the aristocracy. Being their chaperone will be much more difficult, I fear."

"Am I to follow them about like a lapdog?" Hannah sighed. "And my commission! I wrote to Mrs. Pentercast, but I can only hope she will forgive my delay."

Eleanor's honey-colored brows drew together in a frown of obvious concern. "I hate to add one more thing to your list of worries, my dear, but you must know. Farmer Hale, who brings the milk, told me the most awful thing about Brentfield."

"What?" Hannah asked, feeling that brick sinking through her again.

Eleanor bent closer. "You know that Lady Brentfield is widowed? Her husband, the previous earl, and his heir were killed in a coaching accident eight months ago. Farmer Hale told me that he heard from one of the tenants of the estate that it was no accident. When the grooms investigated, they found the carriage had been tampered with. Charles Talent, Earl of Brentfield, and his son Nathan, Viscount Hawkins, were murdered."

Hannah gasped. "Were there no investigations? Did no one come forward with evidence?"

Eleanor reached out a hand and squeezed Hannah's. The warm touch did nothing to ward off the chill Hannah could feel running through her. "Farmer Hale said it was all hushed up. There wasn't any reason for murder, you see. Lord Charles and his son were well liked, and there wasn't a great deal of available money. There wasn't even another heir in England, and when the solicitors traced the family lineage, the fellow they found to inherit was so far removed that he couldn't possibly have planned a murder. I heard he is a Yank, of all things. I don't know what to think, Hannah, but I want you to promise me you'll be careful. This work could be dangerous."

Hannah sighed. "It's dangerous all right—dangerous to my sanity and dangerous to my painting career. I can only hope it isn't dangerous to my life as well."

Two

It took a great deal to anger David Tenant, the soon-to-be confirmed Earl of Brentfield. Those who had known him during his youth and apprenticeship in Boston would have called him even-tempered, jovial, every man's friend. Those who had in turn been apprenticed to his leather shop had been known to term him generous, broad-minded, and fair. The fine ladies of Boston who had been known to praise his carved and colored works of fine leather, smiled at his rakish compliments, telling their friends what a charming and handsome fellow David Tenant was. One month in the company of Sylvia Tenant, the widow of the former Earl of Brentfield, and he found himself wondering whether he was capable of murder.

Her ladyship also seemed to be at the end of her silken rope. She had tried flirtation, she had tried desolation, she had tried seduction. In all cases, he had made it known that he wasn't in the slightest bit interested.

It wasn't that he misunderstood her. From the moment he had arrived at Brentfield to claim his inheritance a month ago, she had been working in the most obvious ways to ensnare him. She had started by following him about with the simplistic adoration she seemed to think men found pleasing, introducing him to the aged estate and telling him how much he was needed to return it to its former glory. He could see that the place did indeed need work. Some of the plaster in the little-used rooms was peeling, and he was afraid the dampness that was the apparent cause might have resulted in some structural damage as well. There were any of a dozen things he needed to do to determine the core of the problem and fix upon a solution, but he found it impossible to move with the lovely widow hanging on his arm. In an effort to keep her occupied, he had commented that she needed a purpose and set her to work inventorying linens. Only later did Asheram, his steward and friend, inform him that one did not set a countess to such a task.

However, her ladyship was not to be deterred. She had then tried flirting outrageously with him, to the point where he was embarrassed to be in the same room with her. Hoping to kindly refuse her, he had lightheartedly asked whether she might be catching the croup, as her voice was decidedly husky and she seemed to have something in her eyes by the way she perpetually batted them. When she had stomped from the room in a fit of pique, he had begged Asheram to find them a suitable chaperone. He was beginning to realize that if he spent too many nights alone in this house with the woman, someone might suggest that he marry her. But the elderly female relative to whom Asheram had written never arrived. David had been forced to move his things to the more dilapidated east wing, putting over a city block between them.

Still, she had refused to give up. Playing the widow grieving over the deaths of her late husband and his only son from an earlier marriage had given her several opportunities to sob on David's shoulders and press her head against his chest. She had sighed long and bitterly over the fate of widows who were inadvertently left out of their husbands' wills. He had patted her on the back, set her on her feet, and assured her she would be well taken care of. Unfortunately, she did not seem to believe him.

He supposed the woman was attractive in her own way. Beneath the powder, rouge, and kohl, she did seem to possess some natural beauty. She was perhaps five to seven years older than he was, yet her golden blond hair was thick and wavy, her eyes a startling blue. She was forced to wear black for her late husband, but the dark silk gowns were designed with tucks, ribbons, and laces, all calculated to bring attention to her considerable curves. He did his best to give those curves as little attention as possible.

Tonight he kept his gaze steadfastly out the floor-to-ceiling windows, looking to the northwest across the grain fields that ringed the great house. He could feel her eyes on his back, as if she could not understand why he found gazing at the view more interesting than admiring her. Her ladyship could not possibly comprehend his fascination with the acre upon acre of rolling Somerset farmland he had inherited. He had never been out of Boston in his life, never been able to see beyond the end of the street he was on. Here he could literally see for miles. He found he never tired of the view. But her ladyship would say that no gentleman should take such an inordinate interest in his lands, beyond knowing that they provided amply for his upkeep.

But he was no gentleman, despite all her attempts to make him into her perception of an earl. Ever since he had appeared at the broad oak doors of the estate, head bared, carpetbag in hand, she had dropped hints, made suggestions, and gently tried to nudge him toward her ideal. He had resisted, feeling as if the woman were trying to take away some substantial part of himself. As a result, he was still dressed in tweed jacket and trousers with a knotted scarf at his throat like some farmer from the field, even though she had insisted he allow a tailor from Wells to build him an entirely new wardrobe befitting his station. He still spoke with what she considered the rough twang of a Colonial, when he could have availed himself of the diction teacher she had recommended. Worst of all to her mind, he knew, he still insisted on walking about the estate daily when he had a perfectly good stable and her offer to teach him to ride.

But she refused to give up her campaign. He had to credit her with tenacity. When she lost on one front, she quickly moved to battle on another. He was not sure what her aim was in joining him here tonight in the Blue Salon, as she called it, but he had no doubt he was going to quickly find out.

"Then you are determined to stay here this Season?" she asked with a suitably regretful sigh.

David looked at her at last and found that she had artfully arranged herself across one of the blue sofas the immense sitting room possessed. Seeing the knowing look in those kohl-rimmed eyes, he found himself thankful that her seduction attempt two nights before had failed. Thank God Asheram had interrupted them, and thank God David was strong enough to resist her blatant pleas to follow her back to her room. The woman thoroughly frustrated him. Sometimes she seemed determined to become his lover, and other times he wondered whether he had anything to do with this lust of hers to remain the reigning Countess of Brentfield. He knew by reviewing the many portraits of Tenants past that he bore some family resemblance to her late husband. He was tall, with dark hair and blue eyes. He had the Tenant nose—long, slender at the bridge, and wider at the tip—although he certainly hoped his own mouth was more expressive than the ones in the paintings. He'd like to think he looked more amused than foreboding, although with her ladyship, perhaps foreboding wasn't such a bad idea.

"Yes, I'm staying," he answered her, once again refusing to use her title. She took a deep breath as if to steady herself, and he wondered what she found in his manner to annoy her this time. She had already lectured him today on his demeanor (he was too familiar with underlings), his choice of reading material (novels, apparently, were for women only), and his vocal projections (his tone was too gentle to inspire the servants, although he seemed to get the household staff to do his bidding more quickly than he had seen them do hers). According to her ladyship, an earl should command, he should sneer, he should bring the world to its knees with only a look. It all sounded like so much nonsense to him.

"But don't feel you have to stay here with me," he felt compelled to add in the face of her disapproval. "I know you want to return to London. I'd prefer to stay here until Asheram and I finish the projects we've started." He carefully avoided any mention of what those projects entailed. He was not about to tell her that his friend's inventory of the Brentfield estate had indicated that several priceless works of art were missing. He honestly didn't think she was behind the thefts, but he wasn't taking any chances until he knew more.

"But you must be confirmed in your title," she protested earnestly. "You must take your place in Parliament. You must make your bows in Society. Do you wish to appear a rustic?"

He shrugged. "I *am* a rustic. How many earls do you know who made their living carving leather in Boston?"

She could not help wincing at the mention of his plebeian background, and he found himself grinning at her. To his mind, it was a kind of honor to rise to the top of one's profession at the early age of thirty and two. Her ladyship and the solicitor who had come to fetch him in America seemed to have other ideas.

"You could show them how much you've learned by coming to London with me," she insisted. He watched as she obviously considered which face and emotion would most sway him—should she hang her head pathetically, or perhaps sniff in true regret? He felt his grin widen even as her eyes widened as she realized he knew her game. She gave up the pretense and tossed her head instead.

"Now," he countered, "how can I run off to London when you've been telling me how much the estate needs a firm hand?"

He had her there. She could hardly contradict her earlier complaints that the place was falling apart without a man to run it.

"You've done so much since you arrived," she hedged. "Surely Haversham can manage in your absence."

David gritted his teeth in annoyance as she once again butchered his friend's last name. "It's Asheram, your ladyship. Mr. Asheram," he said trying once again. "And I wouldn't go anywhere without him." Regaining his equilibrium with difficulty, he winked at the tall Negro gentleman who stood sentinel beside the double doors to the room. "What about it, Ash? Do you have a great desire to see London?"

"Not at the moment," the older man intoned in his deep thoughtful voice. "I spent entirely enough time there caring for the Earl of Kent before he died."

Her ladyship rolled her eyes, and David knew she did not believe the story that Asheram had recently retired from a career as a confidant to British aristocracy. As far as David knew, the story was perfectly true. Asheram's English was far superior to David's and the man's wide-spaced dark eyes were too knowing for a British butler. He carried himself more like a warrior than a servant. He certainly dressed well, in buff pantaloons and a quite respectable bottle-green coat. He even knew how to tie a cravat. Yet her ladyship persisted in treating him as if he were an escaped slave David had rescued from an American plantation.

"There you have it, your ladyship," David concluded. "Asheram and I will be staying here for some time. I'm sure you'll enjoy your trip to London." He started to turn away from her, but she called out to keep his attention.

"I'm sorry to have to leave you alone, my lord," she said with a sigh, "but you know that my niece Priscilla Tate is being presented this year. I promised her mother that I would be her guide. My first husband's brother married the most timid and gentle of creatures. Priscilla's mother would never survive a London Season. She cannot even survive a week with her daughter at home. Besides, my connections are so much better than theirs. And they know I dote on the girl. I will have to go up for the Season shortly after Easter. However, I would not feel right if I did not provide you with some company before then. Anticipating your desires, I have invited a few people over for the week until Easter."

David knew he should be annoyed with her cavalier attitude toward what was now his home, but having guests could only keep her ladyship occupied and away from him. He spread his hands. "Not at all. I'm sure you'll have a fine time."

"If I may ask," Asheram put in, "how many guests is her ladyship considering and when will they arrive?"

She scowled at him. Of all the people on the estate, she had not been able to understand his friend's role in the household. David respected Asheram's knowledge of how the aristocracy managed and had been more than willing to let the man review the papers on Brentfield. His friend had already identified a number of discrepancies between what was supposed to be inherited and what was actually in evidence. He had also uncovered information that indicated that the previous earl and his son might not have died accidentally, as David had been told. To David's mind, Asheram had every right to ask after guests, as he would probably be making the arrangements. Her ladyship apparently realized this as well, for she sighed.

"I invited my niece. I wanted to spend some time with her before we start the Season. And she requested to bring some of the girls from her school—three, I believe.

They are all well connected. Their fathers are all influential."

David could not find it in himself to be as impressed as she would have no doubt liked. She obviously decided it was not worth the effort to pursue that train of thought. "The school will, of course, send one of its staff as a chaperone to assist me. You need not worry about her. They should arrive by the end of the week."

David eyed her thoughtfully. "Is that all? Somehow I thought you'd want something bigger."

She plucked at the silk skirt of her mourning gown. "It is too early for that, I fear. No, Priscilla's company will be sufficient. A young lady on the verge of stepping out into Society is so lovely and untried. She has such a fresh outlook on life. Do you not think so, my lord?" She watched him closely, and David wondered what she was hinting at this time. She was certainly not a young maiden in first bloom, and he had no intention of trying to convince her she was.

"I only hope," he replied, "that your niece won't be disappointed by this quiet country life."

"Priscilla adores the country," she cheerfully replied, and he wondered whether that could be true if she was so close to her city-loving aunt. "I'm sure you'll enjoy her company as much as I do. She plays the piano with the skill of an artist and her singing would stop the birds in envy." Again she watched him, but this time he refused to take the bait. He found it difficult to believe she had stopped throwing herself at him only to throw her niece instead. He purposely returned his gaze to the landscape.

"You will honor us with your attendance at our events, won't you, my lord?" she asked with the perfect note of humble anticipation.

"If I must," he told the view, knowing he sounded rude. "Although I don't think your niece and her friends will have much interest in me."

"On the contrary, my lord," she replied, and he could

hear the smile in her voice. "I'm sure each of the girls will be delighted to make your acquaintance. If you'll excuse me, I should retire."

He did not answer, willing her to leave him in peace. He felt her rise and wait for his acknowledgment, but he had had enough. She let out her breath in frustration and stalked to the door.

"A word, my lady," he heard Asheram offer. "Let his lordship find his own way. He can be quite stubborn when provoked. I'm sure you'd rather have him as a friend than an enemy."

That much was true, David thought, although he didn't want to get that angry with her ladyship. She was a widow, and one beholden to the new earl. He intended to live up to his promise to make sure she was cared for. But he didn't have to endure her criticisms and seductions as part of the bargain.

Her ladyship reacted to the suggestion with her characteristic haughtiness. "I need no advice from a servant. Tend to your own affairs, and stay out of mine."

"The well-being of David Tenant is my affair," Asheram told her. "I owe him my life. I won't let you interfere with his."

He heard a sharp intake of her breath as if she could not imagine anyone talking to her in such a manner. "Remember your place, Haversham or Ampersand or whatever your name is," she sneered. "You may have insinuated yourself into some sort of stewardship here, but I am the mistress of Brentfield. This house was mine before you came and it will be mine again."

David's hackles rose. The woman would tempt him to throw her out yet. "Over my dead body," Asheram murmured. "And David's."

"If you insist," her ladyship replied.

Three

Hannah's dismay at the situation only increased as a few days later she watched her single valise being loaded into the boot of the Brentfield carriage. Each of her charges had a trunk and at least two bandboxes waiting to be stowed, and the girls seemed as restless as the standing horses to be off. Priscilla did not attempt to hide her vindictive pleasure that Hannah had been induced to accompany them. Daphne was fairly hopping in her excitement, Ariadne was green in anxious anticipation, and Lady Emily predicted it would rain before long and turn the roads to mud. Trying not to be out of charity with them so soon in the journey, Hannah turned her attention to the carriage, which was a shiny black with silver accoutrements. The silver and black crest on the side told her that those must be the Brentfield colors. She tried not to be concerned that the emblem on the Brentfield crest was a wildcat rending a stag in twain. Somehow it only reminded her of Eleanor's whispered gossip about the deaths of the previous earl and his son.

The journey itself proved to be almost as troublesome as Hannah had feared, and certainly did not bode well for their week.

"We shall all be crushed inside this carriage," Lady Emily promised after they had bumped some distance from Barnsley. "He'll roll it on the next curve, you wait and see."

"Lord Brentfield's coachman seems quite competent," Hannah assured her, only to bite her lip as the carriage hit another rut.

"I think I shall be sick," moaned Ariadne Courdebas beside Lady Emily. Her gloved hands hovered in front of her trembling lips, and Hannah felt her own stomach lurch just looking at the girl's pale round face. To her relief and the girl's embarrassment, all that erupted was a ladylike hiccup. Ariadne's face turned a healthy pink that matched her pink pelisse.

"I think you're simply excited," Daphne exclaimed on the other side of her, bouncing so vigorously that she set the blue silk ribbons on her pelisse fluttering. She enthusiastically poked her sister in her well-padded ribs, sending Ariadne into Lady Emily and Lady Emily into the equally well-padded wall of the coach. Lady Emily glared, and Ariadne clutched her side as if she'd been kicked by a horse. Hannah sighed and uttered a prayer for patience.

"Well, you should all be excited." Priscilla sniffed beside Hannah. "If it hadn't been for Aunt Sylvia's invitation, you'd all be cooling your heels at the school during Easter holiday."

All three girls colored at the reminder.

"It was very kind of her ladyship to invite all of us," Hannah told Priscilla, determined to put on a pleasant face. "I'm sure a week at Brentfield will be most educational."

Emily grunted, Ariadne grimaced, and Daphne nodded in agreement. Priscilla eyed Hannah thoughtfully.

"You say educational as if we were the ones to be educated, Miss Alexander," she replied, smoothing down the skirts of her lavender lustring traveling dress. "You might find you'll learn something as well. I don't suppose you ever got to go out much in Society before you became a spinster."

It took all of Hannah's strength not to return the unkind remark with one of her own. She was aware that she was on the shelf, but somehow the reminder rankled. Her own mother, widowed at a young age, had tried to raise Hannah and her younger brother Steffen as their knighted father would have wished, but it was clear from the outset that Steffen must receive the schooling and training to make his way in the world. Hannah, it was hoped, would marry a country squire and raise children. But Hannah had fallen in love with her painting. Given the choice of marrying an elderly vicar or finding a post, she had elected to apply for the position of mistress of art at a school in faraway Somerset. Hannah was probably the most surprised of anyone when she had been given the job.

"I'm sure we'll all learn something," she replied to Priscilla, hoping her slight frown would reinforce her meaning that Priscilla had things to learn as well, such as manners. As usual, the subtle look was lost on the girl.

"I don't see how," Ariadne muttered. "Priscilla's already admitted that there won't be any young men."

Hannah shook her head at their obsession. "Come now, Ariadne. There is more to life than flirtations."

At that, they all protested at once, forcing her to hold up her hands in mock surrender.

"But Miss Alexander, how are we to practice for the Season?" Ariadne cried. "We have only a few weeks left before we are presented, and Miss Martingale has yet to allow us a single male on whom to practice our wiles."

"And I'm sick of playing the boy every time we practice waltzing," Daphne put in.

"And I of playing the boy while everyone tries their insipid conversations," Lady Emily grumbled.

Priscilla made a face, somehow managing to look charming at the same time. "There you go complaining again. Isn't a week in the country better than staying alone at school?"

"Easy for you to say," Lady Emily muttered. "You have a beau waiting for you at Brentfield."

Ariadne gasped.

"You weren't supposed to tell!" Daphne scolded.

Hannah glanced around at the three worried faces and Priscilla, who preened. She had a sudden vision of a strapping farmer's son riding up on a Percheron and sweeping the fair Priscilla off to Gretna Green the moment the coach stopped at Brentfield: Hades Carrying Off Persephone. The elopement would surely be followed by the outraged Lady Brentfield demanding Hannah's resignation. Worse, her reputation would be ruined—she might never get another commission.

"Beau?" she ventured, almost afraid to hear the answer.

Priscilla's eyes glowed. "Aunt Sylvia is arranging for me to marry the new earl."

Hannah gaped. "But he's your cousin, and he must be years older than you are."

"He isn't my cousin," Priscilla maintained. "He is a distant cousin of the previous earl, who was my aunt's second husband. My father is related to her first husband. No one even knew the new earl existed until the old earl and his son Nathan were killed in that coaching accident. The solicitors had to search all the way to America for an heir. My mother was certain Aunt Sylvia would have to run the estate herself until they found this fellow. The king even had to waive some law to allow him to take the title. It's supposed to honor the last earl's memory. And the new earl isn't so terribly old. He's younger than Mother."

Hannah opened her mouth to comment, then thought better of it. She could not imagine why a man would want to marry a near-child he hadn't even met. It was certainly natural, she supposed, that he felt some duty toward the widowed Lady Brentfield, but he hardly had to marry her niece.

The description of the chaperone Lady Brentfield had requested suddenly struck Hannah anew. Her ladyship had wanted someone quiet, unassuming, dutiful. Priscilla's confession proved that what Lady Brentfield was looking for was someone who would keep the other girls occupied and provide no competition to the beauteous Priscilla, either in looks or in trying to ingratiate herself with the new earl. Hannah, more interested in her art than Society, was a perfect choice. She wondered whether Miss Martingale had known, or whether Hannah had truly been the only teacher available.

"You see, Miss Alexander?" Lady Emily grumbled. "It's just as I said. She'll spend all her time billing and cooing, and the rest of us will be bored to flinders."

"Lady Brentfield is far too good a hostess, I'm sure, to invite you to no good purpose," Hannah replied, turning to them and hoping she was right. "She must have all sorts of diversions planned for your visit."

Lady Emily looked unconvinced, but Ariadne and Daphne brightened. As graceful as a bird, Priscilla waved a languid hand at the passing scenery.

"You will find out soon enough," she told them. "We are about to enter the estate."

Daphne and Ariadne scrambled over Lady Emily for a view out the carriage window. Only Priscilla sat back in her seat, arms crossed under her breasts. Hannah, however, could not resist a look out her own side of the carriage.

Since leaving the school shortly after Palm Sunday services, they had circled the west end of the Mendip Hills, passing by the village of Wenwood and running over the River Wen. Shortly thereafter, they had passed through vineyards, vines greening with spring. A two-story stone gatehouse now hove into view. The carriage slowed. An elderly man clambered out of the house and set about opening huge wrought-iron gates topped by balls of gold. As the gates swung open against stone columns, the horses sprang through. The man offered the gaping girls a deep bow.

Hannah knew she should sit back in her seat and not gawk like her charges, but she had never seen such grandeur. Majestic oaks crowded on their left and an emerald meadow dotted with jonquils swept away on the right. The meadow led up to the placid waters of a reflecting pond, which mirrored the front of a great rose-brick house. The drive led up over a white stone bridge arching the stream that fed the pond, and onto a circular patch of white gravel encircled by a shorter wrought-iron fence with gold balls on each post. A gate from the drive opened to a garden-edged path that led up to the porticoed porch of Brentfield.

Hannah stared. The walls of the house led off in each direction, three floors full of huge, multipaned windows edged in white. Liveried footmen as smartly dressed as the house strode out to assist the girls in alighting. Grooms sprang forward to hold the horses. The girls crowded past her, giggling and chattering. Hannah was so mesmerized that she didn't even realize they had all left until a footman peered into the coach and started at the sight of her.

"Can I help you down, miss?" he asked. Hannah blinked, then offered him her hand. Her half boots crunched against the snow-white gravel. She tilted her head back, holding her straw bonnet to her head with one gloved hand, staring at the three golden urns that topped the pedimented porch.

"They tell me," said an amused voice, "that the house was designed to mimic Kensington Palace."

"I was thinking of Olympus, actually," Hannah replied. She glanced at what she had thought was another footman and froze. Standing beside her was a gentleman who took her breath away. A Modern David in the Field, her artist's mind supplied, noting the tweed trousers and jacket. She wondered whether she'd brought enough brown with her to capture the warmth of his thick, straight hair. She'd need red for highlights too, or perhaps gold. No, she'd paint his eyes first, a deep, soft blue that would change, she would wager, with what he wore. And she would have to find a way to immortalize that welcoming smile, tilting more at one corner as if her wide-eyed stare amused him.

And she was staring, she realized, although she couldn't seem to help herself. She wanted to commit every detail to memory, as she did before painting a subject. She needed to make note of his earlobes, which were attached to his oval face. She wanted to remember that his lower lip was more full than his upper lip, and both were a seashell pink. There were a dozen other things she needed to note if she was to capture the man on canvas.

"Are you all right?" he asked when she remained silent in study.

He spoke with an accent, a twang that softened his speech. She had heard French, German, and Gaelic at the school, but she did not think this accent was a result of their influence. "Yes, I'm fine," she managed. She glanced about and found that the footmen were tossing down the luggage from the top of the carriage and the boot. The man beside her appeared invisible to the servants, who bustled past with loaded arms. He was equally invisible to the grooms who held the horses. None of them met his eyes as he gazed about. She wondered suddenly whether her bemused brain had conjured him, like a fairy from a mushroom circle, to grant her wish to paint. But no fairy she had ever read about dressed like a shepherd.

"You're the chaperone from the Barnsley School?" he asked politely.

He was making conversation and she was gawking again. She forced a smile. "Yes. I'm the school's art teacher."

A light sprang to his eyes, making her catch her breath anew. "You're an artist? What medium?"

"Oil painting," she replied, a little surprised at his interest. "Although I like charcoal as well. There is a way of shadowing that gives the subject depth." Realizing she sounded as if she were lecturing, she blushed.

"Do you prefer landscapes, objects, or people?" he prompted eagerly.

"People," she answered.

"Classical or portrait?" he quizzed.

She was beginning to feel like the student for once. "Classical," she responded before she could think better of it. Then, knowing how scandalous that confession was, she quickly corrected herself. "That is, I hope to one day paint portraits."

"Have you studied, then?" he asked. "Would you know a classical piece if you saw one?"

Was this some kind of interview? She seemed to remember being asked such questions when she had arrived at the Barnsley School.

"I am self-taught," she told him proudly. "My family did not have the funds to send me to school. But I can assure you I know the Masters."

He grinned. "Then maybe I could show you a few of the Brentfield pieces."

She looked him askance, still trying to determine why he was so interested. She had met so few who were interested in her painting, even among those she painted. "Are you an artist too?"

His smile deepened. "I've been called that a few times. But I work in leather, not paper or canvas." He held out his hands, which she saw were stained brown. His smile faded. "Although my badge of honor looks like it's wearing off. The mark of a gentleman, I guess."

Even with his gentle voice and accent, he made it sound as if being marked as a gentleman was a shameful thing. He shook himself and offered her a smile that was a pale copy of his original. "I'd love to see your work. And I do have a project that I'd like your help on. You'll be staying until Easter, I hope?"

"As long as the girls need me," Hannah replied. Belatedly, she glanced up the drive after her charges. Not a single girl was in sight. She rolled her eyes at her own ineptitude. Her first assignment as a chaperone, and she hadn't even gotten them into the house!

A tall, elderly Negro gentleman in tan knee breeches and navy coat, and with the undisguisable air of command, was making his way toward them. Othello Coming to His People, her bemused brain suggested.

"I'm in trouble now," her companion murmured. "Derelict in duty once again." He heaved a sigh, but the twinkle in his eyes told her he was hardly sorry.

"You're needed inside," the older man said. Hannah wondered why the Tenants would have use for their own in-house leather craftsman, but she felt a shiver of pleasure that she would be able to see him again during her visit. Perhaps she might find a moment to help him with whatever work he was performing.

The older man turned to her with a bow. "You'd be the Miss Alexander for whom the young ladies are searching?"

"She's still beside the carriage, so they can't be searching very hard," her David quipped. "Now, don't glare, Asheram. You wouldn't want to reduce me to a quivering pulp in front of Miss Alexander, would you?"

"Perish the thought," the man intoned.

"Good. Earn your keep and introduce me the way you tell me these Brits insist on."

The older gentleman rolled his wide-set eyes. "If you would be so kind as to tell me your first name, Miss Alexander?"

Her David leaned forward as eagerly as when he had asked about her painting and set her blushing again. "Hannah," she murmured.

"Miss Hannah Alexander," the man intoned solemnly. "May I present David Tenant, Earl of Brentfield?"

Four

David watched as the adorable little thing gasped and blanched. His grin faded as he thought for a moment she might actually faint. He caught her arm as she swayed, but she snatched it back, staring at him as fixedly as she had when he had first encountered her on returning from his walk. Then he had found it flattering. Now he felt downright alarmed.

"Miss Alexander, welcome to Brentfield," he tried, bowing lower than was probably socially acceptable. "Shoulders for a peer," Asheram had explained during one of their many tutorial sessions on the boat over, "chest for a better, and waist for royalty." Well, Miss Alexander was a princess in his book. And she was by far the most interesting person he had met since arriving in Brentfield. With any luck, she would be able to help him confirm his suspicions about the missing art treasures.

His gallantry only served to make Asheram narrow his dark eyes and the lady tremble. She dropped a curtsy deeper than his bow, and he wondered if that made him the Archbishop of Canterbury. "My lord, you are too kind," she said. "Please forgive my impertinence. I didn't know who you were. I promise not to be so encroaching in the future."

David sighed. All he needed was another doting follower. He tried to tease her out of this sudden fear of him. "If by that you mean you'll treat me with the same stuffiness everyone else does, I'll cheerfully put you back on that coach and send you home."

"My lord!" she gasped.

Asheram cleared his throat, and David returned his glare with a wink. "His lordship is inordinately fond of joking, Miss Alexander," Asheram said. "I'm sure you'll give the young ladies good service while you're here. If there's anything I can do to make your stay easier or more enjoyable, you have only to ask. Now, I must insist you join us in the rotunda. Lady Brentfield is expecting us."

David couldn't have cared less what her ladyship expected, but Miss Alexander was biting her lip and looking even more worried. He offered her his arm, and was relieved when she accepted it. She had long-fingered hands, artist's hands, he thought, and her touch on his sleeve was light but firm, for all she looked like she wanted to tremble. He felt oddly chivalrous as they followed Asheram to the front door.

He sincerely hoped she wouldn't retreat into formalities as she had implied. Funny, but Boston society was often cited as the most formal in America. He'd worked for the wealthy, who for all their praises of his work would refuse to acknowledge him outside his shop, let alone invite him to dinner. In his own circle of merchants and artisans, things had been less codified. A man was judged on his intelligence, his character, and his skills. David had never been found wanting in any area. Yet here, just because of a thin and distant bloodline, he was expected to behave as if he had been elevated to the status of demigod. It was downright blasphemous, and he refused to do it.

Still, he found himself wanting a chance to get to know the woman who walked beside him. From the moment she'd looked up at him, those eyes had caught his attention. Wide-spaced in her pale oval face, they were almond-shaped and a deep warm brown finer than any coffee brought from Jamaica. Inside the bonnet she wore, her hair appeared to be as warm and brown as her eyes. She had a pert nose and a generous mouth. Kissable, his assistant in Boston would have called it. The stiff black traveling dress failed to hide her womanly curves. And best of all, like him, she knew what it meant to use her art to earn her keep.

A footman opened the door for them, and Asheram ushered them into pandemonium. When David had first arrived, it had amazed him that the marble-floored rotunda of the entryway to Brentfield was bigger than his entire workshop in Boston. Now it amazed him that four young ladies, three passing footmen, two maids, her ladyship, and some luggage could make the place actually feel crowded.

"Ladies, ladies," Asheram declared, voice ringing to the domed ceiling three stories above. "If I may have your attention. His lordship would like to say a few words."

His lordship would have liked nothing less. However, David resigned himself to playing the part. Reluctantly releasing Miss Alexander, he bowed again.

"Ladies, welcome to Brentfield. I saw that the blossoms were opening on the estate today, but I see the loveliest blooms were here waiting for me."

Two of the girls, a blonde and a brunette who stood side by side, simpered and giggled. The dark-haired one opposite them managed a disdainful half smile. The blond siren batted her lashes at him. Her ladyship glowered, but oddly enough her gaze seemed to be fixed on Miss Alexander, not on him for a change. Miss Alexander looked as if she were going to be ill.

"Allow me to introduce you," her ladyship commanded, stepping to his side unbidden. She inserted herself so forcibly between them that Miss Alexander had no choice but to step out of the way. David wondered if her ladyship would ever learn that he did not particularly need her help.

"Girls, this is David Tenant, soon to be confirmed as the Earl of Brentfield. My lord, this is Lady Emily Southwell, youngest daughter of His Grace the Duke of Emerson." The dark-haired girl curtsied. He bowed.

"I hope this is a pleasant visit," she muttered, her tone implying she sincerely doubted it.

"And these are Miss Daphne and Miss Ariadne Courdebas, daughters of Viscount Rollings."

The two who stood together bobbed, and he bowed again. "Very pleased to make your acquaintance, my lord," the taller of the two gushed. "And may I say you don't look American at all."

"I left my bearskins and bone rattle upstairs," he replied with a wink. She looked interested, but her sister paled, grabbing her back out of reach as if he were carrying some disease. Asheram scowled at him.

"And of course, my dear niece, Priscilla."

The siren glided forward, dipping into a flawless curtsy. "My lord," she breathed huskily, "we're so glad you came to Brentfield."

The tone was warm but the words implied that it was he who was the visitor. He bowed. "Miss Tate. Your aunt has told me a lot about you."

The lanky brunette—Daphne he thought—snickered.

Her ladyship did not spare her a glance. "My dears, there are lovely rooms awaiting you in the west wing near my chambers. I thought perhaps you'd like to tidy up before dinner. We keep country hours here at Brentfield. Dinner will be at six. Haversham?"

Asheram rolled his eyes as she turned his Ethiopian name into English once again. David had to admit that the woman was focused on what she wanted, often to the exclusion of all else and anyone else. He coughed, and she deigned to glance at him.

"I believe you've forgotten Miss Alexander," he declared.

Miss Alexander curled in on herself as if she wished he'd forgotten her too. Asheram motioned the maids and footmen to escort the girls, who flounced out of the rotunda with animated giggles. Miss Alexander bobbed a curtsy and started after them, but her ladyship's voice stopped her.

"Just a minute. Who are you exactly?"

Hannah bobbed another curtsy, eyes respectfully lowered. "Miss Alexander, from the Barnsley School."

"The school chaperone?" Her ladyship frowned. David could only wonder at her animosity. Had he done the poor thing a disservice by keeping her from the girls?

"I'm the art teacher," she gently corrected. "Miss Martingale requested that I accompany the girls as you suggested."

Her ladyship coolly appraised the woman. "You are not what I had expected."

David looked again at the woman who had captured his attention. She was standing stiffly now, as if she expected to be taken off and hung for some crime. His mind flashed to the shiny, overdone beauty of her ladyship and her niece. He felt himself smiling. No, Miss Alexander was clearly not what her ladyship had expected. Miss Alexander was entirely too pretty. And he had compounded the problem by actually paying attention to her.

"I'm sorry if my conduct is not up to your ladyship's standards," Hannah replied with far more composure than David thought she was feeling. "I shall try to be a good chaperone while we are here."

"I don't see that you need to be a chaperone at all," her ladyship replied. "I find my niece's company more refreshing than I had thought. I'm sure I will want to spend every minute in her company. I will not be needing help after all. And I doubt very much that they will have time for art lessons during their visit. Haversham, have the carriage brought around to return Miss Alexander to the school immediately. I'm sure we should not impose upon her time."

Miss Alexander didn't seem to know whether to be pleased or dismayed by this turn of events. Her head turning in her bonnet, she glanced first to her ladyship and then to David. The young teacher was by far the shortest in the room, and David thought she must have felt surrounded. It seemed only natural to come to her rescue.

"I bet we aren't much of an imposition," he observed. "Miss Alexander seems the type to be devoted to her work. If we find her a nice sunny corner to paint in, she ought to be happy here at Brentfield, and then she can be ready to escort the girls back to the school when they are done visiting."

Her ladyship's eyes narrowed, and he hoped he hadn't sounded as eager as he felt to have Hannah stay. Asheram had obviously heard his tone, for he stepped forward to offer a solution.

"Didn't you express a desire to be painted, Lady Brentfield? Perhaps Miss Alexander could be persuaded to try."

Hannah's eyes widened, and her ladyship sputtered.

"Certainly not! I was referring to a real portrait painter, not an amateur!"

David made ready to jump into the fray again, but to his surprise, Hannah spoke up. "Lady Brentfield might be interested in knowing that I've painted Lady Prestwick."

So, she wouldn't defend herself, but she would defend her work. It was much like his own philosophy, and it pleased him.

"Lady Prestwick," her ladyship sneered, "was once a governess."

"Perhaps that's why she was so kind and patient," Hannah replied. "His Grace the Duke of Emerson has agreed to sit for me when he returns from Vienna, and I delayed painting Squire Pentercast and his family to make this trip."

"Well, I certainly wouldn't want to disappoint the Pentercasts," her ladyship proclaimed triumphantly. "Please, Miss Alexander, feel free to return to your work."

Hannah squared her shoulders, and David could feel her relief at being dismissed. She had work to do, he could understand that, work that was most likely far more important than playing nursemaid to a set of untried young ladies. But he and Asheram had been trying in vain to understand what was happening to the Brentfield art treasures, and this woman might hold the key.

"I think she should stay," he proclaimed.

Hannah jumped and her ladyship frowned at him.

"What on earth for?" her ladyship demanded.

They were all staring at him as if he'd lost his wits. Even Asheram wore a frown, as if trying to understand David's thoughts. "I want to be painted," David told them for want of anything better to say.

Hannah blinked.

Her ladyship's frown deepened. "You cannot be serious. And if you are, we will have Lawrence or Fuseli visit this summer." Her tone was dismissive. David had no idea who the people she had cited were, but he imagined they must be famous painters in England. He had no intention of sitting for hours in front of another stiff-necked Brit.

"Why wait?" he countered. "I'm in the mood now. What do you say, Miss Alexander?"

Hannah opened her mouth, and her ladyship started speaking before the poor thing could say a word.

"No, now that I think on it, my lord, you are quite right," her ladyship said. "We must keep her. I will need her. La, what am I thinking that I will have time to be with four vivacious girls when I have to help you with the estate. Please forgive me, Miss Alexander. It has been a long time since I entertained. Not since my dear Charles died." A handkerchief appeared in her ladyship's hand

and she dabbed at her eyes while sniffing. David wondered whether she had ever considered going on the stage.

"Perhaps we should let Miss Alexander make the decision," Asheram put in. Her ladyship's hand froze in mid-dab. David found himself holding his breath.

Hannah glanced about at them all, then held David's gaze. "Lord Brentfield," she said in her quiet voice, "I'm sure her ladyship can find you a suitable painter. I would like to return to the school as soon as possible; however, I promised Miss Martingale, the head mistress, that I would ensure her students are well cared for and well educated. If Lady Brentfield needs me, I will remain."

It was the second time she had looked directly into his eyes, and he found himself captivated. "You don't have to convince me, Miss Alexander. I never wanted you to leave in the first place."

His honesty set her ladyship to sputtering and Hannah to blushing.

"That settled," Asheram intoned, "I believe we have a room ready for Miss Alexander. If you'll follow me, miss."

"I hope," her ladyship managed with acid tones, "that you will not dawdle in the servants' quarters. I'll need you shortly with the girls."

She had obviously meant it as a parting shot calculated to remind Hannah of her place, but David's temper flared. He had never liked bullies, especially those who kicked someone when they were down.

"Asheram," he barked, "can't we do better than that?"

Asheram glanced from her ladyship's determined pout to his own mouth, which was probably just as set. "My lord," he began.

David met his gaze, and Asheram stood taller. Turning to Hannah beside him, he bowed. "There are a number of rooms in the west wing, Miss Alexander, that should allow you to be closer to your charges."

"All of them occupied," her ladyship announced, daring anyone to disagree with her.

"Try the east wing then." David smiled. "I'm the only one in it and it gets downright lonely at times."

Her ladyship gasped, and Hannah stared at him.

"You wouldn't!" her ladyship cried. "You couldn't! My lord, even *you* have to see the impropriety."

"All I see is that I'm a poor host if I put my guests up in the rafters," David replied doggedly.

Her ladyship stamped her foot. "I will not stand for such goings-on! There are impressionable girls in this house! Miss Alexander, you claim to want to be their chaperone. Can you possibly condone sleeping alone, near a man who isn't related to you?"

Hannah raised her head and looked the woman in the eye for the first time. "I'm sure his lordship could be counted on to be a gentleman."

"I'm always a gentleman," David replied, eyeing Lady Brentfield, "as her ladyship has good cause to know."

Now it was Sylvia's turn to blush.

David bowed to Hannah. "Miss Alexander, you will be safe in this house, wherever you choose to sleep."

Asheram cleared his throat, a clear indication that David had overstepped his bounds once again. That was the problem with this earl business—in some areas he could do anything he wanted; in others he had to walk a dangerously narrow path. So far, he simply hadn't gotten the hang of it.

"Miss Alexander," his man intoned, "if you'll follow me. I think we may have one more room in the west wing."

David could not help grinning in triumph. "I look forward to dinner," he called after them.

Her ladyship flounced out of the room in high dudgeon.

All in all, David thought, it hadn't been a bad beginning.

Five

Sylvia Tenant stormed into her niece's room, slamming the door behind her. Even after only a few moments to herself, Priscilla had managed to litter the box bed with dresses, pelisses, and undergarments in such abandon that it was impossible to tell whether the satin coverlet matched the rose-colored bed hangings. Despite the mess, the maid who was trying to clean took one look at Sylvia's face and fled from the room.

"Who is she?" Sylvia demanded of Priscilla, who sat at the rose-skirted dressing table inspecting her flawless complexion in the looking glass.

Her niece turned to her, and even she paled. "Sh-sh-she, Aunt Sylvia?" she stammered.

Sylvia waved a hand. "This teacher, this chaperone you've brought with you. Who is she?"

"I thought you were introduced," Priscilla said in apology. "Her name is Miss Alexander; I think she's called Hannah."

"I don't care what she's called," Sylvia snapped, pacing the room in her agitation. "What I want to know is her background, her connections. Is she anybody?" She kicked a half boot under the maple wardrobe and slammed the double doors shut as well. The woman could not be important! After all Sylvia's careful planning, after all her hard work, she refused to give up her hopes for some sweet-faced spinster from the back of beyond. Was it not enough she had to deal with that Colonial upstart who thought he could be an earl?

If she had thought he had the least understanding of how things were done in Society, she might have tried to reason with him, but it was clear he was too unrefined to realize her needs. She would not have thought it possible, but he seemed no more capable of appreciating what was required to keep her place in Society than her late husband. She had never been able to get Charles to understand that being the Countess of Brentfield held a certain distinction, as well as a certain responsibility. She could not appear in public in the same dress twice. She could not wear the same jewels all Season. Her carriages, furniture, the very houses in which she stayed had to reflect a certain status. She had a reputation to maintain. The only reason she had accepted his offer of marriage in the first place was that she had it on good authority that the Tenants, unlike many of the aristocracy, had the funds to back up their titled consequence. How was she to know that those funds were irrevocably invested in a trust to maintain the extensive collection of artwork that dominated the manor house?

She had begged, cajoled, and seduced her late husband in hopes of convincing him to break the trust, to no avail. Charles had his mind on his hunting. She had sat through endless meetings while his man of affairs and various solicitors attempted to explain the legality of the trust her husband's father had left. One thing was clear; none of them would provide her with what she needed to maintain her place in Society. She simply had to take matters into her own hands. When Charles and his son Nathan had been killed, she had thought she might have some solace, only to find that her late husband had neglected to mention her in his own will. Worse, he had left the free funds that remained to the blasted trust! Convention demanded that she throw herself on the good graces of the next earl. But that earl could not conceive of her way of life.

She was the Countess of Brentfield (she refused to say dowager). She had no intention of giving up the palatial house for a cottage on the edge of the estate. She had less intention of giving up her place in Society to whatever country-bred wife the man managed to attract with his rustic ways. Her only choice was to bring the man under her control, and the sooner the better.

Of course, if she had been able to locate even a few of her late husband's hoarded treasures, she would have hidden them in her bandboxes and decamped for a London town house. Surely the jade statues from the Orient, the ruby-encrusted mask from India, or the gold helmet from the Americas would have fetched her a pretty price from some unscrupulous dealer in town.

She was furious with herself for not noticing that her late husband had spirited the pieces away before his death. She wasn't sure whether he had realized that she had been selling the smaller pieces to augment the misery allowance he granted her, or whether he had put them away for safekeeping while they were in London. Either way, when she had returned to the manor after his death, the only remaining pieces were far too large for her to carry. She had searched the house in vain before David had arrived. Now her only choice was to make David her slave.

By her reckoning, there were two ways she might bring the man under her control. The first was to marry him—that had failed miserably. The second was to marry him to Priscilla, over whom she could exert some control. She could not watch that plan be summarily dismissed just because this nobody earl had taken a sudden fancy to an impossible consort like a penniless art teacher.

Priscilla seemed incapable of understanding the dangers the woman posed. "She is of no consequence." The girl sniffed, dismissing the subject by turning her gaze to her own reflection once again. "None of the teachers at the Barnsley School is of any consequence. Do you think I should wear the pink sarcenet to dinner?"

"Will you focus on the problem?" Sylvia demanded. "Are you sure this woman has no connections? What of her family? Isn't there some Alexander who was a general? What of the Alexanders of Norwich?"

Priscilla shrugged, picking up an ivory-backed hairbrush from the crowded dressing table and pulling it through her curls. "I've never heard it said she was connected with anyone important. Of course, His Grace the Duke of Emerson seems to have taken a fancy to her."

"Is she his paramour?" Sylvia asked.

Priscilla giggled. "Oh, Aunt Sylvia, really! Who'd look twice at Miss Alexander?"

"The earl, that's who," Sylvia snarled. The very thought so incensed her that her pace increased, her hands worrying before her. She could not imagine what the man could see in the woman, especially after he had so studiously avoided Sylvia's own attentions. Sylvia could not believe that she was past her bloom. Thirty-seven years of fulsome compliments, two husbands, and dozens of highly placed lovers had convinced her she was a diamond of the first water. She had never had the least trouble bending a man to her will, until now.

Priscilla's eyes widened. "The earl? What do you mean? I thought you said he was mine!"

"He should be yours. I was certain we could make him yours. Now, I wonder. Be quiet and let me think."

Sylvia continued her frantic walking, long black skirts rustling as she crossed the Oriental carpet. She could not have blundered so badly so close to the start of the race. She had set the course so carefully. She had chosen the one niece who would obey her in all things, whose mind was most like hers. She had instructed Priscilla to bring with her only girls who would play up her niece's considerable beauty. She had carefully instructed Miss Martin-

gale to send the most docile and obedient of teachers.
She had seen many of the cowed creatures who taught
at Barnsley; never had it occurred to her to also request
that they send a dowd, for they were all impossibly plain.
Why she hadn't noticed the quiet beauty of the art
teacher was beyond her. Trust David to notice and be
drawn to it. There had to be something she could do to
stop this attraction before it went any farther.

"But Miss Alexander?" Priscilla muttered, clearly confused. She went so far as to nibble on her large lower
lip. "She really is a nobody, Aunt Sylvia. Miss Martingale
treats all the teachers with the greatest disdain. Miss Alexander rarely gets visitors; her family lives far away. The
only reason Lord Emerson is nice to her is that she told
him Lady Emily has some talent for painting."

Sylvia paused, her mind working. Was the woman intent on climbing the social ladder by ingratiating herself
to the parents of her elevated students? If the woman
sought a position greater than her station, this could be
something Sylvia could use. "She is a sycophant, then?"

"Oh, not at all," Priscilla replied earnestly. "Lady Emily
is quite talented. Her paintings are rather dark and they
usually involve bloodshed of some sort—beheadings, as-
sassinations, battle scenes, that sort of thing—but they are
very stirring. Ariadne was ill after she viewed Lady Emily's
Death of Marie Antoinette."

Sylvia rolled her eyes. "Spare me the details. So, Lord
Emerson is merely grateful for Miss Alexander's teach-
ings, and apparently the woman possesses some talent of
her own or she would not have received commissions.
She does paint portraits away from the school, does she
not? She didn't lie about that?"

It was too much to hope for. Priscilla eagerly confirmed
the fact. "No, indeed. The school was agog when Mrs.
Alan Pentercast asked Miss Alexander to paint the family.
Mrs. Pentercast may have settled for a squire, Aunt Sylvia,
but you know that when she was Genevieve Munroe, she

had the best taste. She was quite the arbiter of fashion in her day. And you know every lady in the area listens to her now. I imagine if Miss Alexander does a good job, her future will be set."

"And yet she refuses to hurry back and do the commission," Sylvia mused, tapping her chin with one finger. "I do not like to think what she finds here of so much interest."

Priscilla smiled complacently, laying down the hairbrush. "Why, us, of course. Until she is sure of her future as a portrait painter, she must dance to Miss Martingale's tune. And Miss Martingale determined that Miss Alexander would be our chaperone."

Sylvia dismissed the notion with a wave. "I cannot believe such a ridiculous tale. As if anyone would pass up an opportunity to advance because of a sense of obligation. It is absurd. No, she saw the light in David's eyes just as I did. She stayed to feather her own nest, you can be sure of it."

"Then send her packing!" Priscilla cried, rising in her seat at last. "You said the earl was mine! I won't give him up for some nobody with paint under her nails!"

"I can't!" Sylvia snapped. "I was insistent that she leave and *he* supported her. She has already gotten some hold on him—how, I do not know. She is pleasant looking in a dark way, but nothing to your beauty. And she is clearly on the shelf. If what you say is true, she has no connections to offer him, no possible dowry. Ohhh!" She threw up her hands. "The man is beyond me!"

"Perhaps she reminds him of the American natives," Priscilla ventured. "I've heard they have a dusky beauty." She bent to peer worriedly into the mirror. "Perhaps I should try less artifice. Perhaps he likes women au naturel."

"Perhaps pigs can fly," Sylvia countered. "Do not change a thing about yourself, my dear. I have yet to find a man who did not mind seeing nature given a helping hand. Besides, we are guessing, Priscilla. If I have learned anything from this last month, it is that one should not guess where David Tenant is concerned. He inevitably does the unexpected. Perhaps he liked the way she laughed. Perhaps he liked her figure, which is rather good. He might even like the fact that she works for a living." She shuddered. "There is simply no accounting for what that man will do. Yet I cannot wait for him to make the next move. For all I know, that man of his is installing her in David's bed as we speak."

Priscilla's eyes were huge in her face. "Do you really think so? I never would have thought it of Miss Alexander. She seems so . . . so wholesome!"

Sylvia eyed her niece thoughtfully. "You truly have seen no previous signs that she is a fortune hunter? She has not shown a tendency to flatter the girls' male relations?"

"She doesn't even notice when we have male visitors," Priscilla snorted. "She's forever at her paints, Aunt Sylvia. I swear it is the only thing she loves."

Sylvia wondered if the woman was misanthropic. "Has she never had a beau?"

"Not since she came to the school," Priscilla confided. "The only rumor that I've ever heard is that she turned down marriage to a well-settled vicar old enough to be her father because it wasn't a love match. Most of the girls thought it quite heroic of her."

"Worse and worse," Sylvia groaned. "So, if she is not loose and not a fortune hunter, she is an idealist. Just the type to appeal to David and just the type to ignore the differences in their stations if she fancies herself in love. There is only one thing for it. We must prove to David that she is unworthy."

"Well, of course she is unworthy," Priscilla snapped. "She is a nobody, as I have been saying."

"And so is he, if it comes to that," Sylvia reminded her. "No, we will have to do better than pointing out her station if we are to deter him. I tried it just now, and only succeeded in getting her installed in the west wing, with us."

Priscilla made a face. "Oh, delightful. Now she will be forever spying on everything we do. I was counting on at least a floor between us!"

Sylvia could not have agreed more. "We have to think of some plan to discredit her. And it must be good, for he is remarkably broad-minded, even for a Colonial. Think, Priscilla. She must have some faults. Does she drink or take laudanum?"

Priscilla wrinkled her nose. "Certainly not!"

"Does she gamble?"

"With what?"

"Has she taken lovers?"

"At the Barnsley School? There isn't a man in miles!"

"Is she prone to hysterics?"

Priscilla shook her head. "There was a villainous spider on Daphne's easel once. Miss Alexander simply knocked it to the floor and squished it with her foot. Lady Emily painted a picture commemorating the event. That one made *me* sick."

"She cannot be perfect," Sylvia maintained heatedly. "The woman must have some fault, some weakness we can exploit to our purpose. Can she be bribed? Would she accept money to leave?"

Priscilla snorted. "I doubt it. I told you, the only thing she values is her painting."

Sylvia shook her head. Try as she might, she could not see how she might use the woman's love of her paints against her. She would simply have to watch until an opportunity presented itself.

"What will you do?" Priscilla wanted to know. "We only have a week, Aunt Sylvia. I thought you said you wanted me engaged before the church bells rang on Easter Sunday."

"And so I do," Sylvia promised. "All is not lost. We

must simply proceed with care. You must do all you can to turn David's attentions back in your direction."

Priscilla smiled, tossing her head. "Oh, that shouldn't be difficult."

"Don't be overconfident! He was obviously interested in your Miss Alexander. I do not know why, but you can use his interest. You need not be pleasant when you're alone with her, but make sure you show David that you admire her. Get him to confide what he sees in her. We can then find a way to discredit her in his eyes and increase your own value."

Her niece pouted. "That sounds like I shall be doing all the work. Aren't you going to help?"

She smiled grimly, and her niece paled again. "Oh, I'll do all I can to make sure Miss Alexander does not get in your way. Miss Hannah Alexander might just find that she does indeed prefer painting to people after all."

Six

Hannah stared at the lavish room to which Mr. Asheram had led her. The mahogany-framed box bed reached to the low gilt-edged ceiling. The hangings flowed with rose, ivory, and jade. The matching carpet under her feet was thicker than the comforter on her bed at the school and easily ten times as big. With the bed, the twin wardrobes, the dressing table, the set of dressers, several occasional tables, a writing table and chair, a chaise longue, and a quartet of chairs near the white marble fireplace, the room held nearly as many furnishings as her mother's entire home in Banbury. It was a room fit for a countess, not a portrait painter and certainly not the mistress of art from the Barnsley School for Young Ladies. She could not shake off the feeling that she had somehow connived her way into such wealth.

It was quite clear to Hannah that the astute Lady Brentfield had immediately seen how useless Hannah would be as a chaperone. There was no other explanation for the woman's instant antipathy. And she had good cause to be annoyed. Hannah hadn't even managed to get the girls into the house! She had conversed with a peer of the realm as if he were a shepherd! Small wonder her ladyship had decided that Hannah should be sent packing.

Hannah knew she should have been relieved at the dismissal. She could have returned to the school, painted the Pentercasts as she had originally planned. But it rankled that she had not been able to manage the girls as had been expected. And Miss Martingale would have been furious that Hannah had proven so inept. The headmistress would see it as a reflection on the school, Hannah was sure. She might dismiss Hannah out of hand. That would surely reflect on Hannah's ability to gain commissions.

So, given the most nebulous of second chances, Hannah had stayed. Lady Brentfield had confessed she might actually find a use for Hannah's services. Lord Brentfield had mentioned she might be useful in some project of his, although she did not believe that he truly desired her to paint his portrait. He had only been trying to find a way out of a difficult situation. Like it or not, she was back to where she had started on this adventure and felt even less happy about it.

A little blond-haired maid in a dress as black and stiff as her own was busy lighting a fire. "Shall I help you change, miss?" she asked, rising.

"Change?" Hannah murmured, glancing about the room again. The only way she would ever feel comfortable in this room was if she were miraculously changed. She did not think that was going to happen any time soon.

"Change for dinner," the maid explained. "All the young ladies be changing."

"Oh, yes, the young ladies." Hannah managed to bring her wayward mind back to her duty. That was why she had agreed to stay, wasn't it? Her reaction had nothing to do with a need to prove herself after Lady Brentfield's criticism of her work. It certainly had nothing to do with a sudden desire to impress the earl. "I should see about the girls," she murmured. She turned to leave and bumped into Mr. Asheram.

"Miss Tate, the Misses Courdebas and Lady Emily are fine," he assured her. "They're all in their respective rooms deciding what they will wear to dinner. I imagine it will take them some time to reach so momentous a decision."

Despite her concerns, Hannah couldn't help but smile. "Knowing them, it will indeed."

"If you won't be needing Clare, I'll send her on."

Hannah shook her head, and he waved the maid away. He started to follow, then stopped, eyeing her.

"Is your room to your liking, Miss Alexander?" he asked.

Hannah glanced about again at the immense room, guilt washing over her anew. "It's beautiful."

"But not what you were expecting," he guessed. "Be assured you are welcome to it. I hope nothing her ladyship said disturbed you."

Everything Lady Brentfield had said disturbed her. Hannah knew she must behave perfectly as a chaperone from that moment on. And she had to forget she was a painter, for a time. She could not let her pride in her work insult her ladyship. "I was not as respectful as I should have been," she admitted with a sigh.

"Neither was her ladyship," Asheram replied. "However, it seemed to me that some of his lordship's comments troubled you the most."

Hannah felt herself blushing. His lordship had been inordinately kind to her. She told herself not to be encouraged by that. He would certainly focus the rest of his energies on his guests. She probably wouldn't get to say another word to him. Still, she hated Mr. Asheram to think that she was annoyed with the earl. "I realized the minute he mentioned the east wing that he couldn't have meant it the way it sounded," she told the man. "He didn't mean to imply he was installing me near his chambers."

"He seldom means anything the way it sounds," Asheram assured her with a sigh of his own. "Lord Brentfield is in the enviable position of not taking life seriously. It is both his most admirable quality and his besetting sin. Some things and people should be taken very seriously indeed. But then, that's my specialty."

"And I think you must do your job very well," Hannah told him, noting the wise eyes, the noble brow. Ancient Sage, her artist's mind suggested. "Mr. Asheram, is it?"

He beamed at her, the first truly happy smile she had seen on him. "Yes, Miss Alexander. It is Mr. Asheram. I'm very pleased you noticed. Now, I'll leave you to dress for dinner, though somehow I don't think that's such a difficult choice for you."

He had meant it as a compliment to her intelligence, but as she shut the door behind him, Hannah reflected that it was a painful truth. The uniform of the school was the ugly black bombazine she wore. Besides her spare uniform and the old lilac kerseymere she painted in, she owned only one other dress, the navy poplin she wore when going to consult with her painting subjects. That she must surely save until a more formal occasion. In the end, she could do no more than to remove her bonnet, smooth her long, straight hair back into her coronet braid, and hope she was presentable.

She felt even more out of place when she joined her charges in the corridor to walk to dinner. Daphne and Ariadne were dressed in light yellow silk gowns that made their hair glow with golden highlights. Lady Emily wore a darker brown that unfortunately brought out the yellow in her skin. The gown was of such a rich material, however, that it gave off a luster of its own. Priscilla had attempted to look demure in a white round gown with tiny pink roses embroidered around the neckline, but as the neckline was rather low and the waist cunningly tucked to accentuate her curves, she only succeeded in looking sensuous. Vestal Virgin Led to the Altar, Hannah thought, then shook her head to clear the vision.

They all asked her opinion, and she managed some phrase that set Daphne and Ariadne blushing with delight. Lady Emily looked skeptical. Hannah turned to find Priscilla considering her with narrowed eyes. When she met Hannah's gaze, she gave a hard smile that somehow reminded Hannah of Lady Brentfield.

"Miss Alexander," she proclaimed, "you look like a proper teacher. I'm sure we can find you a place at the bottom of the table where no one will notice you haven't any other gown."

Hannah gritted her teeth, but kept her lips turned up in a smile as a bewigged footman in the silver and black livery of the Brentfields led them down the long main corridor that spanned the west wing.

Her annoyance with Priscilla's unkind remark quickly disappeared as she glanced around the great house. They passed dozens of doors on either side, some open. Through them she glimpsed other bedchambers, sitting rooms, a music room, and a sunroom. What caught her interest most, however, were the many works of art that decorated each room. There were portraits, landscapes, battle scenes, and still lifes. There were fine ceramics, bronze busts, and rich tapestries. She spotted at least two full-size marble statues. Like everything else at Brentfield, all were massive.

"What an impressive collection," she marveled aloud to Priscilla, who walked beside her. "Perhaps his lordship might be persuaded to give us a tour."

Priscilla eyed her again, and Hannah had the distinct feeling the girl thought she had said more than she intended. "It is better than a museum, is it not?" she finally agreed. "When I am mistress of Brentfield, I'll allow the poor free visits on every other Wednesday."

"Someone should catalog it," Lady Emily muttered. "Otherwise, who knows what the visitors will run off with."

"I don't think anyone would have the strength to carry even one piece," Ariadne argued.

"Well, I think it's glorious, just as you said, Miss Alexander," Daphne enthused. "If you want me to, I'll ask his lordship for a tour."

Priscilla sniffed. "If there is any asking to be done, I'll do it. Though why I should consent to share my time with David with all of you is beyond me. My nature is entirely too generous."

Lady Emily snorted, but Hannah eyed her charge thoughtfully. Priscilla might claim her attachment to the Earl of Brentfield, but Hannah had seen no sign of affection from his lordship when the girl had been introduced. Indeed, Lord Brentfield had not treated her any differently than he had the other girls. If anyone had received undo attention, it was Hannah herself, although that had only been because of his interest in her art. Perhaps Lady Brentfield had requested that the earl keep a proper distance until Priscilla was presented at court and the betrothal formally announced. Or perhaps Priscilla was making it all up to appear important in her friends' eyes. Hannah felt a little wicked for hoping the latter was true. After only one meeting, she liked the new earl enough to wish him a more thoughtful bride than Priscilla Tate.

In either case, she promised herself as they descended a graceful curved stair, she would keep an eye on the matter. Lady Brentfield would surely not approve of her niece taking great liberties with her freedom before the engagement was announced. Hannah had declared her intention of being a good chaperone, and she would follow through.

The footman led them to another immense room, easily three times the size of the cavernous dining room at the Barnsley School. "The Blue Salon," he intoned as he held the door open for them. Hannah could see why the room had been given the name. The satin draping the walls was patterned in fleurs-de-lis of azure on periwinkle. The expansive sky blue Oriental carpet was edged in a navy scroll pattern. The dozen or so armchairs and sofas that dotted the room varied among beryl, mulberry, and lapis. Most of the paintings on the wall were of cool ocean scenes, although the one still life of a young girl was done in russet. The towering vases on either side of the wood-framed hearth were patterned in cerulean. The intense colors made the black piano at the far end of the room glow with cobalt highlights.

Lady Brentfield rose as they entered. The woman was dressed in black as dark as Hannah's, but the cut of the dress and the material were altogether so much finer that Hannah's spirits plummeted anew.

"My dears, how delightful to see you again. You all look lovely. Don't they look lovely, my lord?"

The earl was standing by the huge window overlooking the grounds, which were even now purpling with dusk, the color clashing with the peacock-blue side curtains. He turned at the sound of Lady Brentfield's voice and moved closer, smiling at them all. Hannah's heart started beating faster when she realized that his smile warmed as it reached her. Perhaps she would get to talk to him after all. Lady Brentfield quickly stepped to his side, and the girls crowded forward, forcing his attention to them. Hannah managed a chaperone's smile and dutifully faded into the background.

"I'm sure there are still a few minutes to dinner, my lord," Lady Brentfield assured him. "Would you like Priscilla to play for you?" She waved at the polished black piano.

"Maybe later," David replied pleasantly. "I thought I should get to know these young ladies. Do any of you paint, like Miss Alexander?"

Hannah caught herself blushing as his gaze sought her out again. Ariadne and Daphne exchanged glances as if they too had noticed the look. Lady Emily narrowed her eyes at him.

"Priscilla is quite gifted in that area as well," Lady Brentfield proclaimed. "Didn't you show me the most darling miniature, Miss Alexander, the last time I was at the school?"

"Yes," Hannah replied, trying to think of a tactful way of reminding Lady Brentfield that the miniature had been painted of Priscilla by Lady Emily, in an uncharacteristically sunny mood. But before she could offer anything more, Lady Brentfield continued.

"That is the way with young ladies these days, so very talented. It's their schooling, I am certain of it. What we would do without dedicated teachers such as Miss Alexander, I surely do not know."

"Neither do I," Priscilla announced, batting her lashes at the earl. Hannah looked closer, realizing that the color of the girl's lashes had darkened and what Hannah had taken for a healthy glow earlier was actually well-placed paint. She wondered whether Lady Brentfield would see this as a sign of forwardness and whether Hannah should broach the subject. Surely this was one of her duties as a chaperone. Glancing at her ladyship, she was not entirely surprised to notice the same features. She tightened her lips and said nothing.

"My lord," Mr. Asheram announced in the doorway, sparing her from further ruminations, "ladies, dinner is served."

David smiled at them all again, and moved closer to Hannah, his eyes lighting as they met hers. Hannah froze as she realized he meant to offer to escort her in. Her— the chaperone! Lady Brentfield evidently recognized the look as well, for she pushed Priscilla against him.

"I know it is your duty to escort me as the highest-ranking female," her ladyship told him pointedly, "but I am so pleased to have my niece here that I yield my place to her."

"Some aunts are too kind," David quipped, offering Priscilla his arm. Her head high, her smile tilting in triumph, she let him lead her through the doorway and down the hall to the dining room.

Hannah took a deep breath to steady nerves that were already fraying. Of course he must escort Lady Brentfield. Evidently it was done differently in America. That had to be the reason he'd sought Hannah out. There was no reason for that fact to be so depressing. She nodded to Ariadne, Daphne, and Lady Emily to follow behind the couple. To Hannah's surprise, Lady Brentfield fell in beside her at the rear of the procession.

"Don't they make a handsome pair?" she confided to Hannah with obvious pride. "I vow I will be happy to see my niece so well settled."

So much for the theory that Priscilla was making it up, Hannah thought, nodding in silence. Yet she could not help but wonder why Lady Brentfield had resorted to forcing the earl to walk with Priscilla if he were indeed enamored of her.

"I want you to know that I appreciate the fact that you take your duty as chaperone seriously, Miss Alexander," her ladyship continued. "But I hope you know that I do not stand on ceremony where love is concerned. If my niece and his lordship desire some time alone together, please know it is my wish that you allow them to do so."

"She is your niece," Hannah replied. As Lady Brentfield's eyes narrowed, she realized she sounded critical. "That is, I would not presume to take your place in guiding Priscilla. I will focus my attention on the girls whose relatives are not present."

"That would be wise," Lady Brentfield agreed. "And perhaps we might find something useful for you to do after all. I'm not sure we need any portraits painted, but I will speak to his lordship on your behalf."

Hannah bowed her head in acknowledgment of the kindness, but inside she wondered just how kind Lady Brentfield could be, to Hannah and to the new earl.

Seven

The following morning, five female faces gazed up at David expectantly. He had not been entirely surprised to learn that in addition to granting him vast holdings and a country seat, being made earl had also gifted him with knowledge of everything having to do with the Brentfield dynasty. When Priscilla had requested with nauseating adoration the night before that he take them on a tour of the great house, he had suggested that surely she and her aunt knew more about the place than he did. That suggestion had been met with such an outcry of denial that he had had no choice but to offer to lead the tour, even though he should be attending to estate business. Besides, he had thought, if he conducted it properly, he would be able to steal a little time alone with the charming Miss Alexander. He didn't need an audience when he explained his concerns about the art treasures.

It had been plain to him last night that from the moment the art teacher had entered the blue room, her ladyship was not going to let the poor thing say a word. Her ladyship was also not about to let David start a conversation that involved Miss Alexander. He had made several attempts, and watched with amusement as her ladyship managed to turn every topic around to her dear niece. After a while, he had considered making a game of it, but Miss Alexander's cheeks kept reddening and he didn't like to see her suffer, so he had allowed himself to be cozened and manipulated until he could decently retire for the evening.

Now they stood in the portrait gallery of the east wing. It was ten in the morning, and even though the girls were dressed in white frothy things that couldn't possibly keep them warm in the pale spring sunlight, they looked decidedly tired to him. He kept forgetting what Asheram had told him, that Society in England went to bed late and woke late, with the possible exception of Miss Alexander, who looked quite presentable to him, even if she was relegated to that somber dress. This tour had probably gotten them all out of bed hours early. Certainly Lady Brentfield was still asleep.

If he was any kind of host, he'd show them something better than the portrait gallery. But while there were a number of objects he was sure Miss Alexander if none of the others would find more interesting, the portrait gallery was the quickest way he could think of to rid himself of his entourage. There was nothing more boring, in his opinion, than staring at people you neither knew nor cared about. Even Asheram, the traitor, had refused to accompany him, keeping himself busy with household tasks instead. However, David was already beginning to think that it was he, and not the portraits, who was on display.

"This," he obligingly lied, pointing to the first picture, "is my great-great-grandmother, Hortense Tenant, the fifth Countess of Brentfield."

Hannah frowned, peering closer at the portrait of a silver-haired matron in a medieval gown that pushed her chest up to an unflattering height. As he was soon to be confirmed as the sixth earl, the fifth countess was unlikely to be his great-great-grandmother nor reside during the Middle Ages. But if Hannah caught him in his obvious lie, she politely did not mention it. The girls gazed dutifully up at the picture.

"She looks ill," Ariadne ventured.

"She died of the black plague," David offered. Lady Emily looked interested. Priscilla smothered a yawn.

"And this," he continued with a wave toward the next gilt-framed portrait in the long sunny gallery, "is her husband, the sixth earl."

"I thought he said she was the fifth countess," Daphne murmured to her sister. Ariadne motioned her to hush.

Hannah blinked, but still refused to comment. The man in the portrait was easily twenty years younger than his supposed wife and wearing the cassock of a priest.

"He must have given up his vows for her," Lady Emily muttered to her friends. "They probably tortured him for it."

"The torture would have been in marrying her," Daphne put in with a shudder.

"And now we come to the maternal side of the family," David went on determinedly. He nodded to a portrait on his right of a stiff-backed military fellow with a chest full of medals. "My grandmother, Lady Alice."

Hannah's eyes twinkled, and she compressed her lips tightly together as if to keep from laughing. Daphne, Ariadne, and Lady Emily exchanged looks of bafflement. Priscilla turned to allow the sunlight from the nearest window to highlight her profile.

"Perhaps we've seen enough of the portrait gallery," Hannah suggested diplomatically. "There were a number of lovely pieces we noticed in the west wing, my lord. Perhaps we should start there instead."

Three of the girls perked up instantly. Priscilla was turning back and forth to see if she could catch a glimpse of her reflection in the gilt frame nearest her.

David put on his sternest frown. "No, indeed, Miss Alexander. Asheram tells me that it is British tradition to start in the portrait gallery, and I am a slave to tradition."

"Really?" she quipped, eyebrows raised. He wanted to laugh with her, but it would have spoiled everything.

"Really," he insisted. "There are at least one hundred and eighty-three Tenants on these walls, and I will not rest until I've shown you every one of them."

Daphne groaned, and her sister glared at her. Lady Emily scowled. Even Priscilla rolled her eyes.

"Of course," he offered graciously, "if you ladies have something else you'd rather do, I'll understand. Didn't you want to go riding?"

Now they all beamed at him.

"Riding is a smashing idea, my lord," Daphne proclaimed.

"The fresh air is good for one's constitution," Ariadne agreed.

"I find even the air of the stable invigorating," Lady Emily added.

"I have the most darling riding habit," Priscilla confessed. "I've been longing to show it to you, my lord."

"Wonderful." He smiled. "If you follow that stair at the end of the hall, you should arrive in the rotunda. Yell and someone will arrive. Ask them to lead you to the stables and tell a groom to escort you. I understand we have any number of horses."

They obligingly turned and strolled to the stair, conversation once more animated. Hannah started to go after them, but he caught her arm.

"Won't you be joining them, my lord?" she asked, clearly confused.

"I don't ride," David told her, grinning. "I've never even designed a saddle. It's a waste of good leather, if you ask me."

"But the girls," she protested, glancing toward the now-empty stair.

"Will be just fine," he replied, linking her arm in his. "They will be happier and we will be happier. The grooms seem like nice fellows. I'm sure they'll be happy to take the girls out riding. I bet you already know that you're the only one who'll really appreciate a tour of this place."

"But Priscilla," she tried—out of duty, he thought.

"Has most likely seen it all before. She visits often, I'm told."

The frown on her face told him she was struggling with the idea of neglecting her duty. She sighed. "In truth, my lord," she confessed, "I don't ride either. If you truly think they will be fine without me, I should probably retire to my room until they return."

"Nonsense," David asserted. "I told you I had work for you to do, and since you find yourself free, I'd like you to start right away. There are several paintings that need to be identified. One's by a fellow named Rembrandt."

"You have a Rembrandt?" she gasped.

"It was hidden away. Come on, I'll show you."

The next two hours were some of the most enjoyable he had spent at Brentfield. He took her to a little-used room at the back of the west wing, carefully checking the corridor before he unlocked the door. She gasped again when she saw the pieces piled about the walls. The classical picture of a warrior and a sleeping goddess she identified with awe as being painted by Nicolas Poussin, a rather famous French painter from nearly two hundred years ago. The colorful piece of an open-air festival she told him was done by Antoine Watteau, another Frenchman who had painted in the last century. The fat females cavorting in their all, she claimed with nary a blush, belonged to the Flemish master Rubens. All were the masterpieces he had suspected.

She was just as interested with the other pieces in the room. While she rolled her eyes at the bust some long-ago Tenant had tried to cast himself, she caught her breath at the other bronze sculpture of a rearing stallion. He watched with pleasure as she dared to stroke the marble of a small statue one of his forebears must have stolen from a Greek temple, and grinned as she gazed with wonder at the gold and lapis death mask that had surely been retrieved from an Egyptian tomb.

When she stepped away from the mask, her eyes were serious. "Priscilla said last night that the house should be opened to tours," she told him. "As an artist and an art teacher, I must agree. These treasures should be shared with others, not piled up in a back room. You must put these on display, my lord."

"Only if I can assure their safety," David replied. Although he had only spoken of the matter to Asheram, he somehow knew that Hannah Alexander would understand as well. "I have some concerns about these treasures, Miss Alexander. I found them hidden."

She blinked. "Hidden? Why? Where?"

David grinned at her, feeling as if she would enjoy the mystery as much as he had. "In a series of secret passageways."

She did not disappoint him. Her dark eyes lighted. "The house has secret passageways? Who put them in? Where are they?"

"I don't know who put them in," David told him, linking her arm in his again and leading her out of the room. "But based on their location, I would say they were originally designed so that certain gentlemen could visit certain ladies unseen."

"Really?" she breathed.

He nodded. "But most recently, they seem to have become a storage place for every movable art treasure this house has. And I don't think I've found them all." He escorted her to the sitting room next door, where a large bronze bust stood on a pedestal along one wall. "Look at this piece, for example. Tell me, do you notice anything odd about it?"

She peered more closely at the bust. "The lines are a bit smudged, but perhaps that was the artist's style." She frowned. "And I don't think this was the original base. It is actually rather small for this bust. Look, you can see cracks here under the lintel where the pedestal is beginning to strain under the weight."

She was as sharp-witted as he'd hoped she'd be. "Precisely! Something else once rested on this base, something much smaller. Something that has been moved elsewhere."

"Someone redecorated?" she suggested.

"No one I know of. Lady Brentfield hardly seems the type to notice such things as the placement of statuary. And from what I hear of the hunting-mad Lord Brentfield, he was more likely to be found on horseback than playing with the estate's art treasures. Besides, I've noticed a number of pieces like this. Wallpaper squares less faded than what's around them where a painting has been removed. Cabinets with a circle in the dust showing where a vase or statue once stood. Nails sticking out of paneling where something was hung."

"The russet painting in the Blue Salon," she guessed.

He nodded. "Yes. In general, inferior objects like my ancestor's bust replacing what I bet were finer pieces."

She blanched. "You suspect theft, then?"

"I did at first, until I found the secret passageways. While it's impossible to match things perfectly, by the coloring or the decoration scheme, I can sometimes tell where those treasures you saw used to reside. I bet the rest are still somewhere in the passages."

She frowned. "Just how many passages are there?"

"They honeycomb this place." He grinned at her. "There's even one starting in your room."

"There is?" She looked puzzled. "I can't imagine where it could be. The room is huge." She glanced at him suddenly, then lowered her eyes, a blush creeping to her cheek. "Where does it lead?"

She had every right to be suspicious. Here he was admitting he knew an illicit route to her bedchamber. But being the proper earl wasn't going to solve the mystery of the misplaced artwork. "It connects with other passages at the corner of the west wing," he hedged. "I admit I haven't been through all of them. But in each one I have

been through, I've found at least one of the art treasures."

"I don't see why anyone would hide such work away,"
she protested. "Were they hiding the pieces to come back
later and remove them from the house?"

"Or protecting them from someone else who wanted
to steal them?" David countered. "I don't know. Sometimes these things are tucked into corners or slid behind
beams. Sometimes they're lying abandoned right in the
center of the passage. But I could use help in searching,
from someone who understands what to look for and the
potential value of the pieces. Are you willing?"

As she considered the matter, he led her out of the
room and back down the west wing, stopping before the
door of the room she had been given. He could tell by
the way she bit her lip that she was torn. Already she
understood why the pieces must be found and preserved,
but he wasn't sure she trusted him enough to wander
about in the dark unescorted. Perhaps he should prove
his trustworthiness.

Before she could protest, he swept open the door and
strode to the wall between one of the wardrobes and the
dressing table. Pressing the center of the engraved panel
allowed him to slide it to one side. Hannah, who had
followed him, peered past him into the darkness beyond.
He grabbed a candle from the bedside table and lit it.
Holding it before him, he stepped into the hidden corridor. "Come on. Perhaps if you saw the passages, you'd
understand."

She cocked her head as if considering his motives, and
he gave her his best grin. "I won't bite, I promise. Think
of what you could experience for your next painting."

"I paint people, not dark corridors," she replied, but
she stepped into the space beside him. He slid the panel
shut and motioned her to follow him.

The corridor was tight; they had to go single file. He
was used to the pale plaster on either side, the dust that

piled along the floor, the feeling of clamminess that came over him even though the passage could not have been any more humid than the rest of the house. He wondered what Hannah was feeling, seeing it for the first time. Glancing back at her, he found her gazing about, almost as awed as when he had showed her the masterpieces. He grinned and led her on.

The passageway ran along the south wall of her room for a short distance, ending in a set of narrow stairs.

"Watch your step here," David advised, balancing the candle so that he could reach back to help her. "As we go up over the rooms, you have to walk on the beams."

"Over the rooms?" she questioned, taking his hand to help herself up.

"As I said, it's quite a honeycomb," David replied as they reached the top. He pointed to a two-foot-wide beam that ran off into the darkness. "Make sure you walk on that and that only. Stepping off on either side puts you directly on the plaster. You aren't very big, so it might not matter, but I'd hate to see you fall through."

She swallowed. "Is this dangerous?"

"No, as long as you know what you're doing. This way." He could feel her reluctance growing as they walked the short distance to the corner of the west wing. There the passage opened up into a cross. She blinked at the branching corridors before her. David gestured with his free hand.

"There's one of these at the corner of each wing," he explained. "If you go steadily south along that corridor, you'll find yourself up near the rotunda. Each wing has a spy hole, I assume for viewing arrivals without their knowledge. If you go steadily north along this one, you'll eventually find yourself connecting with the servants' stair at the end of each wing. The servants don't seem to know this maze is here, but I can't afford to believe that until I've recovered all the treasures and perhaps learned why they were spirited away. Going east or west leads you to the descending stair for that wing."

"Amazing," she breathed, eyes wide in the light of the candle. Her concern was obviously lost in the excitement of the unexplored. "I wondered why the ceiling was so low in my bedchamber. The box bed nearly touches it. It made the room seem out of proportion."

He beamed at her. "That's what made me suspect a hidden passage as well. This place is immense; it didn't make sense to have such low ceilings in so many of the rooms, especially when the rotunda has a three-story ceiling. And I hope you can see my dilemma. With one hand holding a candle and being careful to stay on the beam, it's difficult to search. I literally fell into that Rembrandt. Luckily it wasn't damaged. But with you along, I'm less likely to miss or damage something."

The longing in her eyes assured him she was weakening. "Surely Mr. Asheram could help you," she countered.

"I need Asheram to manage things while I'm off searching. Besides, this is an adventure." He paused for a moment, watching her, but he couldn't tell if his point had persuaded her. There was another reason he wanted her beside him, alone with him. Perhaps she should know all. "Let's be candid, shall we?"

"About what?" she hesitated.

"About everything." He stepped closer and gazed down at her. "I'm not very subtle, Miss Alexander. I don't bother to hide my feelings, good or bad. I like you, have done so since I first laid eyes on you yesterday. Aside from the fact that I need your help to find the last of the treasures, I'd like the opportunity to get to know you better. That doesn't seem to be all that proper according to your British traditions."

"And you always go by tradition," she teased.

That she remembered made him smile. "If I don't, there are others who do. Her ladyship, for example, uses traditions as a pawn, remembering them and forgetting them as they serve her. You must have noticed that she doesn't like seeing us together. She won't make it easy for me to spend time with you. If we met in the passages, we could avoid her censure."

She lowered her head before answering. "My lord, you must understand my position," she murmured. "I am honored you find me interesting. I admit that I enjoy your company as well. But I cannot afford a scandal. It is my dream not to spend my life as an art teacher, but to earn my way as a painter. If I make Lady Brentfield my enemy, I could lose everything I dream of. Besides, you and Priscilla have an understanding. I cannot trespass on that."

David started. "Priscilla and I have a what?"

She glanced up at him. "An understanding. Both Lady Brentfield and Priscilla have explained it to me. You have agreed to marry Priscilla Tate."

David started to laugh, then caught himself. The rumor wasn't entirely funny, not when these British took such matters so very seriously. "I assure you, Miss Alexander, that Miss Tate and I have no understanding. I've never met the girl before yesterday, and I certainly haven't talked to her aunt about marrying her. In fact, when I'm with her aunt, I avoid that topic above all things. I don't even call her Lady Brentfield; it makes her sound like she's my wife. I have never been engaged to anyone, either in England or in Boston. I've never even been tempted before now."

She caught her breath, and he realized that he'd said more than he should have. "So you'll do it?" he hurried on. "You'll help me search?"

"If it won't interfere with my duties," she hedged. She glanced about the dark corridors again and shivered. "Are you sure it's safe?"

"Some parts of the house are in poor repair," he allowed. "But I'll show you which areas to avoid. And I'll be with you when we go exploring. If you ever need me between our trips, just follow that corridor to the east. The descending stair ends beside my bedroom."

"I doubt I'll need to go that far," she replied primly. He grinned at her unconscious pun and apparently realizing it as well, she colored. David took her hand.

"Don't worry, Miss Alexander. I promise no harm will come to you. Let me show you around my secret world. You never know what you'll find."

"That's what I'm afraid of," Hannah muttered.

Eight

Hannah had never thought her chaperone assignment would lead to anything remotely enjoyable. She was delighted to find herself swept up into a fantasy world of dark corners and arching passages, led by the most handsome of princes to find a treasure greater than she could have imagined. Wondrous masterpieces lay for her to find, if only she had the courage to search for them. The only sober part of the morning was the thought that she was avoiding her duty and the girls once again. Still, she consoled herself with the fact that they would be well chaperoned on their ride by the grooms, and surely Lady Brentfield would have other activities planned for them by the time they returned.

After a short way into the passage, she released his hand and let him go ahead of her, listening with a smile to his animated description of how he had found the other pieces. She had wondered at first about his motives for encouraging her to wander about alone with him. Perhaps in America things were less formal, but even though she did not follow as strict a code of conduct as some of the teachers, she knew it was expected that none of her students be allowed to be alone in an enclosed space with a man who was not her husband. Of course, those enclosed spaces were usually defined as bedchambers or remote sitting rooms with tempting sofas, not dusty, dank passageways where it was safe only to walk single file.

But she needn't have worried. David was a perfect gentleman. More than that, he was a great deal of fun. He joked and whistled as they poked about uninhabited portions of the house and tiptoed with exaggerated stealth over sections that did contain a busy servant or two. Once they passed within inches of Lady Brentfield, who was ringing a peal over poor Clare. The little blonde was temporarily serving as her maid. From the sound of the stinging diatribe, Clare had done nothing more heinous than forget to set out a matching set of ear bobs. Hannah was sure she must be misunderstanding.

"That's the third maid she's had in the month I've been here," David whispered as they moved over the room. "Her ladyship seems to be quite particular as to what she expects of her assistants."

"I would think someone as important as Lady Brentfield could afford to be particular," Hannah whispered back, feeling a little guilty for helping his lordship instead of the lady. "Among the servants it must be an honor to serve her."

"So much of an honor that Asheram had to triple Clare's pay just to get her to consider a temporary assignment," David replied.

Hannah wondered about this as they pressed onward. Certainly she had already seen evidence that her ladyship was not the sterling example of English womanhood she had been led to believe. For one thing, she had lied to Hannah about Priscilla's engagement to David. She might even have been encouraging the girl to lie about it as well, or lying to the girl by assuring her the engagement was real. Surely her motive was only to see her niece well settled. Hannah had heard stories from the other teachers about young ladies who set traps to lure their intended husbands to the altar. Somehow Hannah had always assumed those traps were laid by women far less alluring and more desperate than Lady Brentfield could ever be, certainly more desperate than Priscilla, who wasn't even out yet. It was all very odd, and she agreed more and more with Eleanor's assessment that a great gulf existed between the lives of the aristocracy and the rest of the English citizenry.

Of course, there were many things about Brentfield she found puzzling, foremost this business with the art treasures. Why would anyone have hidden such precious items away like that? If the previous Earl of Brentfield was the hunter David had indicated, it seemed unlikely he had had the foresight to take precautions against some unknown thief. Yet if he hadn't removed the treasures, wouldn't he have noticed that someone else had? Like the russet painting in the Blue Salon, the changes were noticeable. Then she remembered Eleanor's story of a murder and felt a chill run through her.

"Are you all right?" David asked, turning from his place ahead of her in the passage. "You're awfully quiet all of a sudden."

She smiled—overly brightly, she was sure. "I'm fine. Just wondering why the previous earl might have wanted the treasures hidden." There had been no reason for the deaths to be considered murder, Eleanor had said. For that reason alone, the story should be dismissed. But the art treasures would be worth a considerable fortune. Could the thief have attempted murder so as to have a clear shot at the art?

"As I told you, I can only think of two reasons," David replied ahead of her. "Either he was hiding them to protect them, or he was hiding them to sell them."

"Why would he have to hide them to sell them?" Hannah frowned. "They were his paintings."

David shook his head. "Apparently not. All the artwork is part of a trust, and the estate itself is entailed. Do you know what that means?"

"I've heard the term," Hannah told him. "Doesn't it

mean that it has to go intact to the nearest male relative in direct line of descent from the previous earl?"

"Exactly. From what the solicitor and Asheram have told me, the condition generally applies to large tracts of land. The thought was to prevent the breakup of great estates into successively smaller and smaller parcels with each generation. That makes sense for the Brentfield estate. But the collector of all these lovely pieces of art, the previous earl's father, couldn't stand the thought of seeing all his treasures go should his son turn profligate or start gambling. So he set up a trust to prevent anyone from selling a single piece. So, I'm land- and art-rich, and money-poor."

Another puzzling thing about Brentfield, Hannah thought. Why would a father want to force his son to live frugally in the midst of such wealth? "So, the previous earl may have wanted to sell things without anyone knowing about it?" she guessed.

"Right," David agreed. "Asheram has an inventory that came with the house, claiming to be a full representation of every single item. As you can imagine, it's a long list." He glanced back to grin at her, the candlelight throwing his face into profile and highlighting his lean nose. "We've been checking off the pieces as we find them, but there are still a good number missing."

"And you think they're all up here?" She looked around her at the widely spaced beams and plaster in between. Something caught her eye and she stopped. David stopped too.

"There." She pointed toward the supporting beam across from her. "Something's shining in the passing candlelight."

David leaned carefully over the space between them and the wall. He handed Hannah the candle and then braced one hand on the beam while he reached behind it with the other. Hannah held her breath as he drew a small gold statue into the light.

It was a woman with the head of a cat, holding a flail and a crook and dressed in clothes that spoke to Hannah of the Nile. The statue was no bigger than her hand, but the eyes were of ruby and the ends of the flail glittered with what were surely diamonds. Hannah let her breath out in wonder.

"Well done, Miss Alexander," David murmured. "I've already passed that spot twice and never saw this. You've earned your keep this day."

Hannah felt warmly pleased by his praise. She glanced up at him and saw that he was again smiling at her over the candle. As their gazes met, the smile slowly faded, to be replaced by an intensity in his sapphire eyes that made her catch her breath once more.

"Such hard work deserves a reward," he murmured, leaning toward her. Hannah swallowed, sure that she must have mistaken him. But he bent his head and pressed his lips to hers.

She closed her eyes as the sweetest of sensations rippled through her. His lips were warm and gentle. They brushed against hers with the softness of silk. For so gentle a touch, they seemed to ignite a fire deep inside her that left her trembling. As he withdrew, she opened her eyes and found him regarding her with the most tender of smiles.

"Let's see what else we can find, shall we?" he murmured. Hannah wasn't sure whether he spoke of her heated body or the treasures, but she nodded simply. He retrieved the candle and started forward, the statue tucked under one arm. It seemed to her that his walk was less steady than it had been before. She knew her own knees were shaking. David had been wrong—the passages were dangerous, perhaps as dangerous as the singing of her heart.

Nine

By that evening, Sylvia was once more at her wit's end. With David distracted by her niece, or so she had thought, she had slept in and then spent the remaining hours of the morning planning her campaign in detail. The maid Clare had informed her that Priscilla and the girls had gone riding, and it had never occurred to her that David had not accompanied them. It appeared to her that David was proving susceptible to Priscilla's wiles after all. If she was right, all she need do was to find ways to bring the two of them together so often that he would propose by Easter. If the man proved his usual stubborn self, she would simply arrange for her niece to be placed in so compromising a position that he would be forced to marry the girl. Priscilla would owe her place in Society to Sylvia, and Sylvia had no doubt she could control the girl to the point that whatever Sylvia wanted, Sylvia would have. Her future was secured at last.

Her confidence began withering at lunchtime. Although David appeared from one wing and Miss Alexander the other, it was apparent to Sylvia by the glow in the woman's eyes that she was already falling under his spell. When Priscilla chided him for not joining them for a ride and he and Miss Alexander exchanged surreptitious glances, Sylvia gritted her teeth. When Daphne maladroitly proposed a toast to their gracious host and

David's eyes remained on Miss Alexander as he raised his glass, Sylvia groaned inwardly. When David offered them a tour of the back gardens and the girls looked less than enthusiastic, Sylvia kicked her niece under the table.

"Priscilla, you mustn't deprive yourself of this treat," she scolded the girl, who wiggled in her seat as she tried to rub her sore leg. "You've always adored walking about the estate. Perhaps you've finally found someone else who loves it as well."

"Do you walk much when you're at school, Miss Tate?" David politely inquired.

"Whenever possible," Priscilla dutifully assured him. Sylvia caught the art teacher frowning from her place at the foot of the long table, but Priscilla was batting her lashes to effect and David was for once attending. "It is so lovely to feel the cool breezes across one's skin."

The comment should have been titillating, but David turned easily to the art teacher. "And do you take walks too, Miss Alexander?"

"When I have pleasant company." She smiled at him. "Miss Pritchett, the literature teacher, often goes out with me. Otherwise my duties prevent much exercise."

"Always dutiful, that's our Miss Alexander," Sylvia sneered. "You needn't feel bound here, my dear. Walk as much as you like, all the way to the edge of the estate."

"I don't think she need go that far," David declared. "She could start by joining us this afternoon. I promise you I'm better at pointing out plants than portraits."

Again they exchanged knowing smiles. Sylvia seethed.

She managed to divert Hannah from the walk by claiming to be rethinking the need to be painted. Accordingly, Sylvia forced herself to glance through the woman's sketchbook, which she had actually brought with her, making kind remarks about the charcoal sketches. She was surprised to find that they were actually rather appealing, although she could not imagine allowing the woman to do one of her. She had far too many things to do to tie herself to sitting for a portrait. However, that the art teacher would let herself be taken away from her pursuit of the earl by something so innocuous as a possible painting commission only confirmed Priscilla's assertion that the woman loved her paints above all else.

She tested the theory a bit by commenting on one of the drawings, which showed the head and shoulders of a wistful-looking woman gazing off in the distance. "You seem to have a way with drawing, Miss Alexander. You must love it above all things."

The woman had smiled, but it was not a smile of self-satisfaction. It seemed to Sylvia to betoken some sort of melancholy. "I think sometimes I learn more about myself than my subjects when I'm painting, your ladyship." She seemed to recollect her place suddenly and blushed. "But of course, I'm here to serve you. I'm so sorry I was unavailable this morning. His lordship asked me for help with a project, and I did not feel I could refuse."

"No, of course not," Sylvia purred.

The woman looked startled, but Sylvia made a show of turning the page and drew her attention back to the sketchbook.

With Miss Alexander effectively cornered, Sylvia looked forward to an afternoon in which Priscilla would be constantly in the earl's company. Unfortunately, it was apparent when they rejoined the group that neither David nor her niece had been pleased by this turn of affairs. Sylvia knew Priscilla was making a good attempt; she would not dare to do otherwise knowing what Lady Brentfield expected. But it was becoming increasingly clear to Sylvia that the girl simply hadn't the experience to carry off such a flirtation. What had started out as amusement on David's handsome face had turned to annoyance. She was glad when they all had to leave each other to change for dinner.

Priscilla fared no better at dinner. Sylvia was nearly nauseated by the tender glances and inclusive quips David kept throwing in the art teacher's direction. Try as she might, Sylvia was unsuccessful in getting either the conversation or the attention to refocus on her niece. By the time the fruit trifle was served, Priscilla's eyes were stormy and Sylvia feared her niece would have a temper tantrum before the night was out.

Sylvia decided to go all out when they regrouped in the Blue Salon after dinner. She stationed her niece at the piano and set her to playing an American tune that she felt was sure to capture David's attention. She thought perhaps she had succeeded at last, for when he appeared in the doorway, his face split in a grin and he took a seat as close to the instrument as he could. She nodded to Priscilla, who moved on to a more difficult piece. Her playing was flawless, and David's applause genuine and enthusiastic when she finished.

"You play beautifully, Miss Tate," he commented. "That's a gift few can claim."

Priscilla's blush had nothing to do with the rouge on her cheeks. "Thank you, my lord. Would you like to hear something else?"

"Oh, must it always be ballads?" Daphne complained, and Sylvia wondered how she could silence the irritating girl. "Can't we have something more interesting?"

"A battle hymn," Lady Emily suggested, "or better, a dirge."

"Oh, not a dirge," Ariadne protested. "Something brighter."

"A waltz, perhaps?" Hannah put in.

David nodded, rising. "A waltz would be perfect. Do you know one, Miss Tate?"

"I know several," Priscilla bragged. She launched into a particularly stirring one. Ariadne tapped her foot to the beat. Even Lady Emily nodded along. Daphne leapt to her feet.

"Oh, if only we could dance!"

David bowed to her. "Miss Courdebas, I would be delighted if you'd join me."

She ogled him. "Really!" she squeaked.

"Curtsy, you idiot," her sister urged sotto voce.

Daphne dropped a deep, wobbly curtsy. "I would be
honored, my lord."

David took her in his arms and began to swirl her
around the Blue Salon. The room was huge; there was
plenty of space between the piano at one end and the
nearest grouping of chairs in which to take a turn. Sylvia
hurried to the piano and slid in next to her niece. "Make
sure you're next," she murmured, taking over the playing. Priscilla swallowed, but rose obediently and went to
stand beside her friends.

After only a couple of turns, Daphne stumbled. David
caught her easily, but after a few more steps, she broke
away from him, blushing. "I'm sorry, my lord. I'm still
learning."

He bowed again. "I'm sure you're a delightful pupil,
Miss Courdebas."

Sylvia nodded at her niece, and Priscilla stepped
eagerly forward. David turned to Hannah. "Miss Alexander, as you're a teacher, perhaps you'd be willing to dem-
onstrate to your students how it's done."

The little art teacher rose gracefully, black skirts nearly
purple in the candlelight, and dropped a deep curtsy.
"With pleasure, my lord."

David's smile was tender as he pulled her into his arms.

Sylvia's fingers cramped into claws on the keyboard
while she watched them. Hannah glowed with happiness.
David's eyes never left her face as he swept her about the
room. They moved perfectly together, bodies in tune to
each other and the music. Sylvia felt hot anger burning
inside her. She fumbled a chord and watched with satisfaction as David hesitated, spoiling the symmetry of the
dance. She broke off suddenly and snapped the case
down on the keyboard.

"This instrument is out of tune," she announced, rising. "Either that, or I simply don't have my niece's ability with it. Who's for a hand of whist?"

David had no choice but to relinquish his hold on the art teacher, and it galled Sylvia further that he was so obviously reluctant to do so. Still, she managed to get him partnered with Priscilla for the game and set herself up with Lady Emily as partner. Asheram had joined them at some point during the waltz, and he organized the Courdebas sisters and Miss Alexander into another group. In this way, she was able to keep David away from the woman until it was time to retire.

She was certain everyone was asleep when she went to see her niece that night. She had surreptitiously watched to make sure the art teacher was doing her duty for once. The woman had carefully checked on each of the girls before retiring herself. Sylvia had waited long enough to imagine she heard snores from the nearest guest chamber before hurrying to her niece's room. To her surprise, she found all the girls crowded on Priscilla's bed in their wrappers, comparing notes from their visit. She scolded them all soundly and sent them to bed, vowing to give Miss Alexander a similar scold in the morning. Was the woman so naive as to believe that the girls would stay in their rooms after she had seen them to bed? She should be more watchful. Doing her duty indeed. The woman was spending her time making eyes at her betters, just as Sylvia had predicted. Well, it would stop tonight. By morning, David Tenant would be safely engaged to her niece.

"Is something wrong, Aunt Sylvia?" Priscilla asked when they were alone.

"Not if you count losing everything you've ever strived for," Sylvia countered. "You are not attending to your purpose, my girl. You should spend more time with David and less with those children. Honestly, Priscilla, how can you delight in these nonentities? None of them has a brain in her head."

"That's not true," Priscilla replied defensively. "Lady Emily is a great painter, as I told you. And Ariadne is kind, for all she is forever sick of something. And Daphne is clever, for all she cannot make her way without stumbling. I should have known she would never make it through a waltz with a real man."

"You didn't even get a dance, so I would not crow if I were you. Is that your best nightgown?"

Priscilla blinked at the non sequitur, then glanced down at the lace confection she wore. "No, it just felt comfortable."

"Comfortable isn't good enough." Sylvia strode to the dresser and rummaged through the drawers. She tossed a silken gown at the girl. "Put this on instead."

Priscilla crawled out of the bed and did as she was bid. Her slight frown told Sylvia she wondered what was going on, but Sylvia's mind was moving too quickly to allow her to explain. As her niece tied the satin bows that held the gown closed in front, Sylvia stepped behind her and pulled a brush through the golden curls. Then she stepped back in front of her and peered into the perfect face. "You'll do. Come on."

"Where?" Priscilla asked meekly as Sylvia pulled her to the door.

There was no one in the corridor, as was customary at so late an hour in the country. Sylvia towed her niece down the wing and across the central block. As they approached the east wing, Priscilla hurried to match her step.

"This is it, isn't it?" she whispered to her aunt. "He's asked for me?"

"He hasn't the brains to appreciate what's placed before him," Sylvia replied, glancing about before approaching David's door. A light glowed under the panel; he was still up. Biting her lip, she wondered how she might slip the girl in unseen.

Priscilla tossed her head. "Then why do you insist upon

this? I promise you, Aunt Sylvia, we have only to wait until my Season and I'll catch you a duke!"

"A bird in the hand," Sylvia muttered. "Besides, most of the dukes I know do not have funds to rival the Brentfield legacy. He has no refinement. It should be a matter of a moment to get him to ignore the trust and sell this beastly art. Now, be silent while I think."

"Oh, really, Aunt Sylvia! If we're going to do this, let's get it done." Before Sylvia could stop her, the girl reached for the door handle. Sylvia slipped back into the shadows, trying to drag her niece with her. Priscilla shrugged out of her grip and boldly opened the door. "My lord? I'm having trouble sleeping. Can you help me?" She scowled, turning to her aunt. "He isn't here."

Curiosity got the better of Sylvia. Pushing Priscilla aside, she peered into the room. It was empty. A lamp glowed on the bedside table, where a book lay open. A fire was dying in the grate. The bed was turned down and appeared to have been rested on. But his lordship was not in evidence.

With a hiss, Sylvia shut the door. Priscilla took one look at her face and quailed. She did not speak as she followed Sylvia back down the corridor.

He was with *her*. Sylvia was sure of it. Small wonder the woman could not be concerned with her charges. How he had managed it so deftly so as not to be seen by the other inhabitants of the west wing, she was not certain. But managed it he had. She toyed with the idea of exposing the woman, but was afraid it would only force David to play the gallant and marry her. Surely he would not marry her otherwise. Even David had to see the danger of wedding such a nonentity. He was already virtually an outsider to English Society. He must marry a polished woman, someone who would ensure his entrée. This was only an affair, a momentary diversion.

Yet what if the art teacher became pregnant? David was entirely too noble. No, the situation was serious. She had only two choices that she could see. She had to rid herself of the art teacher immediately, or she had to rid herself of David Tenant. She smiled suddenly, and Priscilla hurried to her own room as if to escape her.

Perhaps the best thing that could be done, Sylvia realized, was to rid herself of both of them, once and for all.

Ten

Hannah of course knew nothing of what Sylvia had tried the night before. Hannah had been arguing with herself since she had awoken at a very early hour that morning, and she was still arguing as she approached the breakfast room in the west wing.

She knew she was not the most practical of females. It had not been practical to reject Reverend Timken's kind offer of marriage to take a job teaching school when she had never been particularly fond of children. It had not been practical to agree to postpone a most promising commission to play chaperone, but it had seemed the only solution at the time. It was terribly, horribly impractical to be falling in love with David Tenant, yet she seemed to be doing just that.

When she had gone to bed last night, she had scolded herself for her attitude. She had known him less than two days, for all that it felt like a lifetime. Even when he had said in the passage yesterday that he liked her and wanted to get to know her better, she had not let herself hope beyond a friendship. He was an earl; she was a nobody. He certainly couldn't marry her, and she did not think he would insult her with an offer of a carte blanche.

Not that she would have agreed to be his mistress even if he had asked. Her mother was the daughter of an Anglican minister; Hannah had been raised to a strict set of principles. She sometimes thought her grandfather's reference, rather than her talent with canvas, had been the deciding factor in her being accepted to teach at the Barnsley School. "All our teachers are of stiff moral fiber," Miss Martingale had informed her on her first day at her post. Since then, listening to the sometimes spiteful gossip and bickering of her colleagues, Hannah had wondered whether that fiber was actually straw. Still, she tried to live her life according to the guidelines her mother and grandfather had laid out for her. Becoming David Tenant's mistress was not compatible.

But it would have been so delightful. She allowed herself a shiver of pleasure as she remembered his kiss in the passage. He seemed to have been as affected by it as she was, yet he had not pressed his advantage. In every way, she found him charming. His clever teasing made her smile at his audacity. He was open and honest, a refreshing change from Miss Martingale and most of the other teachers, for whom life seemed a series of posturing and petty grievances. It seemed to her already that she knew what he would say before he said it. She had never felt so comfortable with another human being.

Dancing in his arms last night had felt so right. She had wanted to pull him closer, she had wanted to feel her heart beat in time with his, she had wanted to bask in the warmth of his smile forever. She shook her head to clear the feelings that crowded her. She could not be in love! It was ridiculous. She was destined to be a painter. It was not as impressive as a countess, to be sure, but she might achieve some stature of her own. Two of the painters in the Royal Academy were women. She would enjoy David's company, help him find his art treasures, and be on her way.

She turned the corner of the west wing, and he fell into step beside her as if he belonged there. After her recent thoughts, she dared not look at him. Surely her face was flaming. Just knowing that he had to have been waiting for her made her heart beat faster. Silently he handed her a single red tulip. She lowered her head in the pretense of examining it, anything to avoid his eyes.

"Asheram tells me her ladyship and the girls have been invited to lunch at Prestwick Park. Plead a headache and stay back with me. We can go exploring."

Although it sounded suspiciously like a command, the tone was beseeching. Her heart longed to obey, but she knew she couldn't. "I really must start putting my duty first, my lord. Besides, I wouldn't feel right misleading Lady Brentfield."

She glanced up to find that he was regarding her steadily. It would have been a contrite look if she hadn't seen amusement lurking in the depths. "I'm leading you astray, aren't I, Miss Alexander? You could neglect your duty all day for all I care. It's for a good cause. You yourself said the art treasures should be shared. To share them, we have to put them back in their rightful places."

"But with your guests gone for the day, you can surely take Mr. Asheram with you," she pointed out. "You don't really need me."

The grimace he made looked more like a pout. "But it will be more fun with you along. I told you, I'd like to get to know you better."

"In a dark, dusty passage?" she accused him. "My lord, you do protest too much."

He hung his head sheepishly, and had they been outdoors, she would not have been surprised to see him digging a hole in the dirt with his toe. "But I really do enjoy your company, Miss Alexander. I guess when I'm interested, I continue to move forward until I succeed or hit a brick wall. Did I hit a wall?"

Was he truly interested in her? Was he actually attempting to court her? Suddenly all her ruminations seemed to be unimportant. David Tenant, the Earl of Brentfield, wanted to get to know Hannah Alexander better. David Tenant might actually be falling in love as well. She stopped in shock, and he stopped beside her. Looking up into those vivid blue eyes, the half smile on his tender mouth, the determined set of his chin, Hannah swallowed. "No, my lord," she whispered. "You have not hit a wall."

His smile softened. "I'll see about a special lunch. Go in without me. I'll join you in a moment." He took the tulip from her unresisting fingers and brushed the soft petals across her lips. The touch reminded her of his silken kiss in the passage. As if in promise, he pressed the flower to his own lips in salute. Then he strolled away. Warm from head to toe, Hannah floated into the breakfast room.

The room, relatively small by Brentfield standards, had a wall of windows facing the morning sun. The bright glow exactly suited her mood. Lady Emily actually smiled as Hannah took her place next to the girl at the oval table that graced the room. Ariadne and Daphne called greetings from across the table as well. The only one who looked at all unhappy was Priscilla.

The beauty slouched in one of the scroll-backed cherry-wood dining chairs, perfect lips compressed in a decided pout. The apple muffin that lay before her on the Wedgewood china had not been touched. Hannah could easily attribute the girl's sullen glances in her direction to Priscilla's usual preoccupation with herself. Clearly the girl was not getting the attention she thought she deserved, which was all of it. Although Hannah felt a twinge of guilt, she knew it was time the girl learned to share.

It was Lady Brentfield's manner, however, that most surprised her. The dowager countess sat complacently behind her cup of chocolate, paying little attention to the conversation that ebbed and flowed around her. But she lifted her eyes and smiled when Hannah seated herself, asking after her health. Hannah had expected anything from a ringing denouncement to complete snubbing by the woman. After all, Hannah had been monopolizing their host's attention, something the dowager could like even less than her niece did. Yet Lady Brentfield was charm itself. She even encouraged Hannah to partake of the succulent strawberry tarts that lay on the sideboard along with the other delicacies prepared for their morning meal. Hannah shook her head.

"Tea and toast are all I find necessary in the morning," she assured the countess. A footman obligingly brought her a cup and plate.

"Are you sure, Miss Alexander?" Ariadne exclaimed, blue eyes gazing fondly at the tempting pile of pastries. "They look wonderful to me."

Lady Brentfield reached out to pat the girl's hand. "I'm certain they do, dear, but you must consider your figure. Miss Alexander is of an age where a few more pounds do not matter. You, on the other hand, still expect to attract a mate."

Ariadne colored, clearly crestfallen, and Hannah busied herself with spooning honey into her tea. She hoped no one noticed how her hand shook. Another morning, the stinging comment would have reduced her nearly to tears. At the moment, all she could think about was how unkind the remark was to Ariadne.

"Besides," Lady Brentfield added as if she had not noticed the havoc she had wrought, "those are his lordship's favorites. I'm sure you wouldn't want to deprive him of his pleasure."

"I wish someone would," Priscilla muttered.

Despite herself, Hannah frowned. There was an undercurrent here. Both Lady Brentfield and Priscilla were out of countenance, for all that her ladyship kept smiling. Hannah only hoped she was not the prime cause of the anger.

David chose that moment to saunter through the doorway, his smile of welcome somehow blotting out all the unpleasantness of the last few minutes. Hannah smiled in return as he helped himself to an orange off the sideboard. She noticed Ariadne watching him as well as he considered the tarts. The girl pouted as he turned without taking one, and Hannah had no doubt that if Lady Brentfield left before Ariadne did, the girl would stuff herself.

"Good morning, ladies," he greeted them, seating himself at the foot of the table and setting about peeling the orange. Hannah watched his long-fingered hands tear into the meat with as much fascination as Ariadne had watched the tarts. "What are you doing today?"

Three pairs of eyes looked expectantly at Lady Brentfield. Priscilla yawned. Hannah stiffened, knowing that she would soon have to fulfill her promise to David and lie. Lady Brentfield's manner notwithstanding, Hannah wasn't sure she had it in her.

"We've been invited to lunch at Prestwick Park," Lady Brentfield announced. "The Earl of Prestwick is most particular as to who visits. We are quite fortunate."

The three girls managed polite smiles, but Hannah could tell they did not appreciate the honor.

"Besides"—Lady Brentfield smiled, raising her cup of chocolate—"Lord Prestwick is very handsome, extremely rich, and quite unattached."

Instantly, Hannah's charges were preening, all except Priscilla, who rolled her eyes. Hannah wondered what there could be about the purportedly handsome earl that would make him uninteresting to the normally predatory Priscilla.

"I haven't met the earl yet," David mused, pulling off a wedge of orange. His tone was interested, and Hannah thought perhaps he had changed his mind about staying behind. Disappointment coursed through her, and she told herself she should be grateful that she would not have to lie.

Lady Brentfield apparently heard the interest as well, for she hurriedly responded. "As I said, my lord, Lord Prestwick is most particular. I think it best that only the

girls and I attend." She turned to smile over-brightly at
Hannah. "Which means we won't be needing your services either, Miss Alexander. Feel free to paint or do whatever you like."

The last few words had a decided edge on them again,
and Hannah caught herself blushing even though she really wasn't sure why.

She spent the rest of the morning helping the girls
prepare for their upcoming luncheon. It was rather amazing to her that it took over three hours to dress and coif
four young ladies. The choice of gowns alone took over
two hours, with much trooping from room to room to
match ribbons to gowns and gowns to pelisses and
spencers and spencers to shoes. She was quite glad to
stand in the rotunda and wave them all good-bye.

David, who had joined her for the farewells, turned
eagerly to her as the footmen shut the doors. Mr.
Asheram offered Hannah a smile.

"I understand his lordship has a job for you," he intoned, and she realized he said it as much for the footmen's benefit as to make conversation. "I'm sure you'll
do quite well."

"I'll try," Hannah assured him.

He nodded. "I've always found serving Lord Brentfield
a privilege."

David clapped him on the shoulder. "Listen to him.
You'd think he'd been serving me for years. And he
wouldn't be 'serving' now if I had my way about it."

"Someone has to see to administering the estate," the
older man reminded him.

"And glad I am that that person is you," David
quipped. "What is it today, Ash, taxes or tithes?"

"I am still attempting to inventory the house based on
the previous earl's will," his friend replied. "So, in my
own way, I'm also helping with your work. I'll go over my
findings with you later as you requested." He nodded to
David and bowed to Hannah, then disappeared into the

back portions of the house. Hannah let David lead her forward.

They spent the next hour wandering about the passageways. Unfortunately, they found not a single piece of art.

"Are you sure there are still more missing?" Hannah frowned as they came out in the west wing. "Perhaps you've found them all."

David shook his head. "I don't see how. There are still several paintings and a number of smaller pieces that look to be missing, according to the inventory list. How about if we break for lunch and try again later? I got Mrs. Abbot to make us a picnic lunch. Will you join me?"

Hannah nodded, suddenly shy. "But won't your servants talk? I thought you wanted to avoid Lady Brentfield's censure."

He looked thoughtful. "I suppose someone might notice at that, although I get the impression most of the servants like Asheram and me better than they like her ladyship. Why don't you pretend to be drawing in the sunlight in the garden? I'll meet you and we'll make our escape."

She grinned at him. "Sometimes, my lord, you are entirely too inventive. I'll get my cloak and bonnet."

His plan worked, and soon they were strolling down a country lane toward the fields beyond the house. The day was bright, the fields showing signs of spring. Green tufts of winter wheat turned formally barren ground to an expanse of ocean that rippled in the breeze. Clumps of crocuses dotted the edges of the lane they followed, and jonquils waved above the new grass. David walked beside her, knapsack slung on his back. When he reached for her hand, she gave it gladly.

He chose a spot on the lee of a gentle slope, the field rolling away before them until the wheat ended in a stretch of wood. The oaks were stiff and dark, a line of winter across the hope of spring. She set her back to the

view of the trees and opened her sketchbook as he spread
a plaid blanket on the ground.

"All this is yours, then?" she asked as he pulled bread,
cheese, and fruit from the knapsack. Her hand strayed
across the surface of the open page of her sketch book,
and she had a sudden desire to draw him. She watched
his profile, strong yet gentle. It would be a challenge to
capture so complex a gentleman. The idea was heady and
she found that her hand trembled. She shut the book
and reached instead for the food he had set out.

"As far as the eye can see, or so they tell me." He
dug out a silver flask and poured wine into two tin cups.
They were dented and scratched, and somehow she did
not think they had come from the Brentfield kitchen.
"Everything you see belongs to Brentfield, except for
that stretch of wood. Supposedly that marks the dividing
line between the estate and the lands of Prestwick Park.
I've been trying to find the records that show exactly
where. I even wrote to the Earl of Prestwick, but he
hasn't answered. He probably suspected I was trying to
take more than is mine. That's more likely the reason
he hasn't introduced himself, not her ladyship's excuse
of my lack of pedigree."

"I don't understand the reference," Hannah confessed, hackles rising at the thought of how cavalierly the
countess sometimes treated David. "You are a Tenant,
aren't you?"

"Is that with a capital T?" he teased. "Yes, I'm a Tenant, but I had no idea I had relatives still in England, let
alone in the aristocracy. My four-times-great-grandfather
came to America over a hundred years ago, and his
grandson settled in Boston in time to start the tea riots.
If we had aristocratic roots, they were burned right then
and there. And with me being a leather worker, by her
ladyship's standards, I'm not even good enough to be a
merchant. I'll simply have to marry above my station."

The bread was harder to swallow than she had thought,

and she washed it down with a draught of wine. "Yes, I understand."

He set down his own slab of bread and cocked his head, eyeing her. "That was a joke, Miss Alexander. I'll marry whom I like."

She felt the color flooding her cheeks again and bowed her head. "Of course you must do as you see fit."

"That," he murmured, cupping her chin and tilting her head up so that her gaze was forced to meet his, "is the most sensible thing you've said all morning."

It took everything she had to pull away. "I seem to be having a difficult time being sensible where you're concerned," she admitted.

"Then stop trying," he quipped, winking at her. He took a mouthful of the bread and chewed contentedly. The breeze ruffled his silky hair. She could easily marry this man. But joke as he would, he needed to marry an aristocrat if he was to be accepted socially. Hannah squared her shoulders.

"Do you have any idea how dangerous this is?" she demanded.

He raised an eyebrow. "Dangerous? To whom? How?"

"To both of us! You asked that we be candid, my lord. Surely you can see the difficulties coming. The very fact that you feel we must hide our meetings proves as much. Gentlemen may be able to laugh off such clandestine meetings, but we women have our reputations to consider. Even in America there must be some expectations of young ladies having chaperones."

"You're a chaperone." He grinned. "I have never felt safer."

Hannah threw up her hands. "Will you be serious? Do you want a reputation as less than a gentleman?"

"I am less than a gentleman," he reminded her, not unkindly. "And rather proud of it. And I assure you I won't breathe a word of any of this to anyone, except perhaps to our grandchildren."

Hannah caught her breath, but he merely winked at her again and went on munching. "Tease," she told him accusingly.

He grinned again. "Better to laugh than to cry. Besides, you English worry too much." He leaned back on his elbow as if to prove that he was immune to such petty concerns.

"Not so!" Hannah felt compelled to defend her country. "It was our Andrew Marvel who said, 'seize the day.' "

"A man after my own heart," David proclaimed. "Tell me, Miss Alexander, what day would you seize if you could?"

She could think of one at the moment, but didn't dare voice it. "I'd study classical painting. And I imagine you're one of the few that won't be shocked by that fact."

"Not particularly," he admitted, taking a sip of wine. "Should I be?"

"Oh, my, yes. In classical painting, the models are nude, you see. It isn't considered proper for a woman to view nudes."

"Only to stand as a nude model before male painters," he quipped.

"Ah, but those aren't ladies. Still, I'm not unhappy being relegated to portraits. People are so fascinating to study. I think I shall be quite good at it, if I ever get the chance." She realized she was bragging, and blushed.

"I'd like to see your work," he declared. "Do you have any pieces in your sketchbook?"

She breathed a silent prayer that she had not yet started to draw him. Surely the picture would confess her feelings. "A few." Shyly she pushed the book at him. He set down his cup and began to thumb through the pages. Abruptly he stopped, peering closer. The next few pages were turned slowly and thoughtfully. Hannah held her breath.

When he glanced up at her, his face was more serious than she had ever seen it. "These are very good. I can almost imagine I know these people. I could care about them. You have a gift, Miss Alexander. You must use it."

"I intend to," she replied, and at that moment, she meant it with all her heart. His praise warmed her, all the more precious for its rarity. He nodded, returned the book, and resumed his contented munching.

All too soon, he declared it time to return to the house. "We still have our exploring to do," he reminded her when she protested. He climbed to his feet and offered her a hand to help her up. As he pulled her to his side, she found herself against his chest, his mouth scant inches from her own. She did not so much as blink as he moved to close the distance.

Eleven

"Miss Alexander!"

Asheram's call broke David's concentration, and he jerked up before his lips could meet Hannah's. At the foot of the hill behind them, he saw a carriage and horses. Asheram was climbing the hill. Although a moment ago she had looked so tender that he had longed to kiss her, Hannah now thrust herself away from him as if he had burned her, and smoothed down her skirts. She looked as adorable as she looked guilty. He winked at her, and she blushed.

"Miss Alexander," Asheram panted as he reached them. "You must return with me. Miss Ariadne Courdebas has taken ill."

The blush disappeared as quickly as it had appeared. "Oh, dear, I was afraid of this. It's probably just an upset stomach, but she's forever thinking she's dying of some dread disease. I'd better see what I can do."

The fierce look on Asheram's face told David it was useless to argue. He bent and crammed the remainder of their lunch back into the knapsack. "I'll come with you." They hurried down the hill to the vehicle.

Based on Hannah's words and his own assessment of the girl, David was surprised to find on their return that Ariadne appeared to be quite ill indeed. She lay ensconced in the huge bed of the room she had been given, her normal rosy complexion a ghastly white. The bright light in her eyes told David she was delirious.

"I'll send for a doctor," he promised Hannah, who immediately took off her bonnet and cloak to help the maid minister to the girl. David thought about staying as well, but Asheram motioned him out into the corridor. Hannah offered him a regretful smile as he left.

"I've sent Weimers for Dr. Praxton," his friend explained. "I'm sure Miss Alexander is capable of handling the girl until he arrives."

"She shouldn't have to," David snapped. "Where's everyone else? Her ladyship seems only too happy to play hostess around here until someone gets sick."

"Lady Brentfield and the other young ladies are downstairs while her ladyship's and Priscilla's things are moved to the east wing. Her ladyship did not want to take the chance that this illness was contagious. She has a Season to consider."

David snorted. "But it's all right to expose the other girls and Miss Alexander?"

"Would you like me to remove their things as well?" Asheram asked, not unkindly.

"Not until we're certain this is dangerous. You saw the girl, Ash. What do you think?"

To David's surprise, his friend looked up and down the corridor before drawing David farther from the open door. "I think Miss Courdebas may have been poisoned."

"What!" David cried. He quickly sorted through possibilities, then shook his head. "You've been listening to her ladyship, Ash. The Earl of Prestwick may be a bit miffed with me, but you can't think he'd poison an innocent girl. What would he gain by it?"

"You assume it was the earl. From what the young ladies tell me, Ariadne began feeling unwell on the carriage ride over. They cut short their visit when her condition worsened. She collapsed before they reached Brentfield. I suspect she was poisoned at breakfast."

"But by whom and why?" David persisted. He peered more closely at his friend. From the first moment he had met Asheram on the boat from America to England, the older man had impressed him as levelheaded and responsible. The London solicitor who had found David had insisted that David take one of the two main cabins, himself going to sleep with the other passengers in the hold rather than disturb the very important dignitary who supposedly had reserved the second cabin. He had been shocked to find that Asheram had been that dignitary. David had found it amusing that the solicitor continually tried to put the man in his place and Asheram continually rose above it. David's easygoing nature had endeared him to Asheram. The older man's serious demeanor had been a challenge to the irrepressible David, until he realized that Asheram's stiff comments often carried a biting humor. He could see no sign, however, that his friend was trying to make light of the current situation.

"Ash, this doesn't make any sense," he protested. "How could Ariadne have been poisoned under our noses? Mrs. Abbot had over a dozen dishes on the sideboard at breakfast. All of us ate some of one thing or another. Yet Ariadne is the only one sick."

Asheram sighed. "David, you must believe me. This isn't a joke. I'm beginning to suspect that Lady Brentfield is dangerous."

"Lady Brentfield? Her ladyship isn't even dangerous in whist," David countered. "Oh, I might tremble if I had a daughter looking to get married. I have a feeling her ladyship could be vicious if she thought Priscilla's place was being threatened. But Ariadne Courdebas is no threat to her. Priscilla is three times as beautiful, four times as talented, and, I shudder to say, twice as intelligent. No, Asheram, I refuse to believe I'm in any danger from her ladyship."

"Very well. I'll try another direction to get through to

you. Will you believe you're in danger from Hannah Alexander?"

The thought was so ridiculous that David gave it up and laughed.

Asheram shook his head. "You simply can't see it, can you? How can a man so wise in the ways of the world be so stupid when it comes to self-preservation?"

David raised an eyebrow. "Just who was it who got so caught up in a poker game that he bet his own freedom?"

"But I nearly won!" Asheram protested earnestly. When David continued to eye him, he stuck out his chin. "Very well. You've made your point. Cards are my weakness, and they would have gotten the better of me that night if you hadn't interceded. I don't know what came over me to want to play with the crew. I will be forever in your debt. Let me return the favor. This dalliance with Miss Alexander is dangerous—to both of you."

His words were remarkably like those Hannah had uttered on the hill that afternoon. He had heard the excuses about his reputation, and he rejected them. "How am I endangering her?" he asked, eyes narrowing.

"That got you, didn't it?" Asheram chortled triumphantly. "You refuse to think of your own well-being, but you'll think of hers."

"Answer the question."

"Very well. I know you too well to think you're playing with the woman. Although if you were, I might point out that you will ruin her reputation, and she will never get another teaching post or a decent painting commission again."

"I'm not playing with her, as you put it," David growled, knowing his annoyance was out of proportion for Asheram's fatherly advice. "I need her help to locate the art treasures. And I like her." He paused, remembering their kiss in the passageway the day before. He wasn't sure why he had taken that liberty with her, but her sweetness had stolen his breath away. Already "like" seemed far too subtle an emotion. He shook himself and continued. "I'm not out to take advantage of her. My intentions are honorable."

"Just as bad. You may not understand the social customs here yet, my lad, but I've seen far too many of these mixed-class marriages. She'll never be accepted as your countess. Even your children, if you have any, will have a devil of a time."

"Then I'll take her back to America," he replied defiantly, "where she'll be respected for who she is and not her fancy title or lack of one."

"And leave the estate untended? You've objected to that from the first, or so you told me."

"You know I have," David snapped. "I didn't want this title, but when the solicitors assured me that the estate would be returned to the crown, and Lady Brentfield and the two hundred farmers evicted if I refused, I had to accept. It was my responsibility, Asheram."

"And a weighty one it is, to be sure," Asheram agreed. "You can see for yourself that the place badly needed your leadership. Even with the improvements you've planned, there'll be little enough income for the first few years. But that could change, if you married well."

"Marry for money? I'd sooner sell that death mask."

"Go around the trust and denude the estate of its treasures? Would you leave your sons less than you were given?"

"At this rate, I won't have sons to worry about," David countered. He ran a hand back through his hair. Glancing across the corridor through the open door, he could see Hannah bending tenderly over the sick girl, wiping her forehead with a cool cloth. He returned his gaze to Asheram, and knew his voice sounded as desperate as he felt. "All my life I waited for the right woman, Asheram. I'd watch my assistants and friends fall in love and marry, one by one. I even tried courting a couple of times, but no one ever stirred my heart. Now, just when my luck is turning, you want me to walk away because 'it just isn't done'? To hell with your fine British conventions. If I decide to marry Hannah Alexander, I'll marry her."

"Stubborn," Asheram growled. "There's more of an earl in you than you want to admit. Very well. I've had my say where Miss Alexander is concerned. You make a fine couple."

The last was so begrudging that David found his anger melting. "Yes," he agreed with a chuckle, "I think we do. Stop worrying, Asheram. Just let me do things my own way."

"I'm beginning to think I have little choice in the matter," his friend quipped. "But don't think you've won me over completely. I reserve judgment on Lady Brentfield. She is lethal, and I wouldn't turn my back on her if I were you."

David clapped him on the shoulder. "With you at my side, she doesn't stand a chance."

Dr. Praxton, a small pointy-nosed fellow, took that moment to arrive, and Asheram ushered him in to see the patient. David waited in the corridor long enough to hear the man's diagnosis.

"She no doubt ate something that disagreed with her," he pronounced. "I've left some laudanum with Miss Alexander to be used should the pain persist. Give Miss Courdebas nothing but clear broth, weak tea, and toast for a couple days and the girl should be fine."

Asheram had shown the doctor to the door, but David checked with Hannah before going downstairs to inform his other guests. He found her sitting at Ariadne's side, reading the Bible to the drowsy girl. She rose and hurried to meet him.

"You saw the doctor?" When he nodded, she continued. "I should stay with her. For all her imaginings, she is rarely truly ill. I think it's frightened her badly. She tells me she had visions. It sounds rather beastly. Perhaps you could have Mr. Asheram send up a dinner tray for me?"

David took her hand and raised it to her lips, warmed by her care for her charge. "I'll bring it up myself."

He left her blushing.

He had to admit, as he headed downstairs, that he rather liked the way the tiniest compliment brought the rose to her cheeks. Not the least arrogant, that one. Her understanding of art, self-taught at that, proved she was sharp as well. Her ladyship had lived in the house for five years, and she had apparently never realized there were secret passages, yet Hannah had caught on right away. And Hannah was far kinder and more thoughtful toward the visiting girls than her ladyship, who had invited them there in the first place. Hannah Alexander was definitely a rarity among the few British woman he had met so far. In fact, he couldn't think of a single thing at that moment that he disliked about her.

After the loyal scene in the upstairs bedchamber, the blue room was a disappointment. The remaining girls were huddled in chairs near the windows, while Lady Brentfield reclined on the divan across the room, calmly shuffling through correspondence. She seemed completely immune to their worried glances and hushed conversation. The girls scrambled to their feet, calling out their concerns, as he entered. Lady Brentfield's gaze flickered up momentarily, and he would have said that the only thing she felt was annoyance at the interruption.

"Dr. Praxton has been here," he explained to the girls. "It isn't serious. Miss Courdebas will be feeling better in a day or so."

"I told you she was pretending," Priscilla sniffed, tossing her head so that her golden curls fell in artful disarray.

"I wish she wouldn't be so missish," Daphne sighed.

"Is it contagious?" Lady Emily wanted to know.

"No," David replied, eyeing Lady Brentfield and remembering Asheram's warning. "In fact, it appears she was poisoned."

The letters slipped from Lady Brentfield's fingers as if they had suddenly gone numb. Priscilla gasped. Daphne trembled. Lady Emily looked grimly fascinated.

"What do you mean, poisoned?" Lady Brentfield asked slowly, as if her breath was held tightly in her chest. She rose from the couch and stood staring at him, ashen. It was an interesting reaction, but not, David thought, necessarily indicative that she had had a hand in the deed. He suspected that any hostess would react so to the news that one of her guests had been poisoned.

"Something at breakfast didn't agree with her," David said by way of explanation. "To her, it was a poison. Evidently, the rest of us were immune."

Lady Brentfield closed her eyes for a moment and opened them again. The blaze of resentment was quickly masked, and David wasn't sure whether it had been directed at him, or the situation. "Thank goodness," she breathed. "I had Haversham move our things to the east wing to be certain Priscilla would be safe. She has a Season to consider, you know."

The other girls, who also had Seasons to consider, exchanged glances but said nothing. Lady Brentfield continued as if she had not noticed.

"I feel almost foolish having him move the things back so soon. I suppose there's no harm in Priscilla and me staying in the east wing for a day or two."

David managed a tight-lipped smile. The last thing he wanted was them next door. He didn't want the secret passage to be discovered, and he certainly didn't want a repeat of the night he had found her ladyship draped across his bed. "I bet your niece would rather be near her friends, seeing as we still have six days left in their visit. I'm sure Asheram won't mind having to move things twice in one day. It's amazing how quickly he accomplishes things."

She did not return his smile. "As you like, my lord. He is your servant."

"He is my friend," David reminded her.

The girls looked puzzled, but her ladyship rolled her eyes. "In any case, we should probably inspect the kitchens to make sure no one else becomes ill. I shall instruct Mrs. Abbot to throw out anything that was left over, just to be on the safe side."

"Wise precautions," David agreed. "I'm sure we'd all like to think this incident won't be repeated."

Lady Brentfield smiled sweetly at last. "Yes, I'm certain you'd like to think so, my lord."

Somehow, that did not make David feel any more comfortable that the issue was resolved.

Twelve

Sylvia had already decided that David was hopelessly plebeian, had no sense of the proper place of things, and was denser than clotted cream. She was not entirely surprised to find that he annoyed her as well. His sense of humor had always been questionable, but his joke that afternoon about the poisoning had been impossible. For a moment she had actually thought he knew of her handiwork.

She was quite glad she'd had the foresight to dispose of the strawberry tarts after breakfast. Her only mistake had been in assuming that the two missing ones had been eaten by David. She had failed utterly in getting that insipid art teacher to try one, but David was by far the more important of the two. She had set out for Prestwick Park hoping she would return to find him writhing on the floor in agony. She wasn't sure there had been enough black henbane in only two tarts to do him in; but if she had calculated the amount of the poison correctly, he could have, with any luck, succumbed before the doctor arrived. And if anyone had questioned his death, she would have blamed it on Hannah Alexander, claiming the woman as his slighted lover.

Now she had to come up with a second plan. Poisoning was no longer a viable option. Two illnesses would be too much to be overlooked. It would have to be an accident, and one that she could be reasonably sure would claim only David. What a pity he didn't ride—it would have been the work of a minute to slice his saddle girth partway through or lame his horse. If he even liked to drive the many estate carriages, she would also have had an easier time. She already had experience in tampering with carriages. Trust David to be so eccentric as to offer her few opportunities!

But much as she longed to put the next plan in place, she had to stop the blossoming romance with Miss Alexander first. The man was so besotted that he had actually ignored his other guests to take her a supper tray like the veriest servant. He was obviously out to convince her he wanted her. They would be lovers in no time, if they weren't already. If he got her with child before Sylvia succeeded in doing him in, and if the child were a boy, Miss Alexander could claim a secret marriage to gain the estate for her son. As desperate as the solicitors would be to find a male heir, they just might overlook the need for evidence, or even help the woman manufacture the evidence if they were properly bribed. No, the safest thing for all concerned, Sylvia decided, was to keep Hannah Alexander away from David.

She considered again what possible hold she might have over the art teacher, and finally decided to appeal to the woman's love of painting, since Priscilla seemed convinced that Hannah had few, if any, other vices. Not that Sylvia would ever have given up a chance at an earl for so silly a pastime as painting, but Miss Alexander did seem ridiculously idealistic. Accordingly, Sylvia stopped by Ariadne's bedchamber before retiring.

Miss Alexander had had a cot erected in the room so that she might sleep near the ailing girl. Sylvia found it hard to believe that anyone would be so loyal, but she could not think of another motive. The Courdebas were not as influential as she had led David to believe, so their good graces would avail the woman nothing. And in Sylvia's opinion, the woman would do far better by being with her lover rather than trying to impress him with her kindness.

As Sylvia entered, she saw that Hannah was already changed into a blue flannel nightgown with a high neck and long sleeves. It did drape her curves well, but it was far from alluring, to Sylvia's mind. Miss Alexander hadn't even had time to take down her braided hair. Sylvia wondered how David would react if he could see the woman gowned so plainly. Of course, even the art teacher's day dresses were hopelessly unfashionable and plain, and he hadn't seemed one whit less attracted. There simply was no accounting for taste.

"Good evening, Miss Alexander," Sylvia announced, closing the door behind her. "I just wanted to make sure you had everything you needed." She glanced at the bed and saw that the girl was sound asleep and drooling on her pillow. She hastily looked away.

"I'm fine, thank you, your ladyship," the art teacher replied with a quick curtsy. *At least she has some sense of her place,* Sylvia thought with satisfaction.

"And Miss Courdebas," she asked, stifling a yawn, "how is she faring?"

"She was given some laudanum and appears to be sleeping soundly," the woman replied, nodding to the girl in the bed.

"How thoughtful of you to stay with the girl," Sylvia murmured, eyeing the rather lumpy cot. "I'm sure if my niece were ill away from home, I'd want someone to care for her as diligently as you are."

"You are too kind," Hannah replied, blushing.

"Not at all," Sylvia assured her. "However, I realize things look different from your perspective, my dear. While I am certainly not old enough to be your mother, I believe I have seen more of the world than you have. So, while you are at Brentfield, I hope you know you can come to me with your problems, just as the girls come to you."

The woman kept her eyes respectfully downcast.
"Thank you, Lady Brentfield, but I have no problems."

"Oh, but you do," Sylvia replied, a sneer breaking
through. The woman's head came up, and Sylvia hastily
modified her tone. "Your situation troubles me, my dear.
You know I held hopes that his lordship and my Priscilla . . . well, that simply wasn't to be. Fate stepped in.
He is obviously smitten with you."

Hannah shook her head, but Sylvia moved to still her
protest. "Oh, but he is. I've had my share of admirers,
Miss Alexander. I recognize the signs. He is quite smitten.
And you, if I am not mistaken, are equally enthralled."

The art teacher said nothing, lowering her gaze once
again. This time Sylvia did not think humility had anything to do with it. "I realize the earl is dashing," she
commiserated. "A more charming man you could not
find. But surely you see the danger in this infatuation.
You must go carefully, or you will lose all you hold dear."

"What do you mean?" she gasped.

"Precisely this: You cannot paint and be his lover. If you
marry him, you will have your hands full running this
household. He certainly doesn't know how to do it, and
Haversham is getting old. The burden will fall on you, my
dear. Believe me, I have seen it happen all too often. You'll
have to manage the servants here, pay the bills, and see to
the tenants' well-being. And the entertaining." She paused
to cluck as the woman grew ever more pale. "Brentfield is
known for its lavish parties. You'll have dozens of visitors
at Christmas, during the summer, and throughout the
hunting season. You'll have to keep them housed, fed, and
entertained. And they are much more demanding than
your current charges. Why, even I tremble at the prospect.
I don't see how you could ever find time to paint."

The woman swallowed, somewhat convulsively, and
Sylvia continued, hammering away at her points. "If you
do find time to paint, you will never be accepted as a serious
artist. You will simply be an oddity, your works tossed away

as soon as the notoriety of a countess craftswoman fades. Do not expect to see any of your things hung in a gallery or prized for a collection. It would be a shocking waste of your talents, my dear. If you were not so sure of your duty to these girls, I would advise you to leave now, before you are tempted."

"Lady Brentfield," she managed, "I appreciate your advice, but I must do as I see fit." Her tone was firm, but her eyes were troubled. She would have difficulty sleeping that night. Sylvia turned away to hide her smile of satisfaction.

"Of course you must, my dear. I leave the decision to your sense of loyalty to your craft. I know you'll make the right choice. A talent such as yours would be a sin to waste."

She left Miss Alexander biting her lower lip and deep in thought. That deed done, and rather nicely, she felt, even with her gross exaggerations, Sylvia checked to make sure everyone else was asleep before making arrangements for the next day. How nice that the house was still in poor repair. She had only to help matters along.

She had decided to keep Miss Alexander under closer watch. Accordingly, just after breakfast, she sent a maid to take the teacher's place in the sickroom. When Hannah reported as commanded, Sylvia was rather pleased to see that there were dark circles under her eyes as if she had not slept well. In fact, the art teacher looked wan and pale and completely unhappy. Sylvia congratulated herself on her ability to motivate people, and set the woman to instructing the remaining girls in the art of watercolor painting.

Sylvia herded the girls firmly into a sunny room overlooking the east garden and set them about their task. Luckily, she had found paper and paint left from a previous house party. Of course, none of the girls, including the supposedly talented Lady Emily, looked the least bit pleased about the activity, but Sylvia did not let that deter her. She ignored their frowns, even the pout posed by her niece. Priscilla would have plenty of time for riding once the horses, and everything else on the estate, were back in Sylvia's control. It would take the solicitors months, possibly years, to find another male heir, if indeed there was one to be found. During that time, she would see to it that every last piece of art on this estate was sold for a pretty price. When the new earl finally arrived, or the crown awarded the estate to some pompous admiral, she would be living well in London on her proceeds.

Her next task was to rid herself of the ever-present Haversham. For this she needed an accomplice. The only other person in the area that she had any use for was the local merchant Mathias Delacorte, through whom she had been selling her purloined pieces of art. It was the work of a minute that morning to send him a note instructing him to appear at the kitchen door at precisely eleven and attempt to barter goods with the steward. She doubted that Haversham would actually buy anything from the man—the steward had been making all his household purchases in Wells. Still, all Delacorte had to do was keep the man away from the library. Sylvia would do the rest.

She also arranged for some letters she had previously intercepted to be delivered to David, forcing him to retreat to the library to review them. He and Haversham had set up a sort of study in a corner of the library, where they pored over the estate papers. The desk was hopelessly covered with books and folios and vellum; she could not see how they accomplished any work, confirming her suspicions that they retreated there to avoid her. Of course, David had been preoccupied the last few days and had not gone near the room.

Before she had resealed the letters, she had confirmed

that the requests they contained, information about his confirmation as earl, were convoluted enough to keep him busy for some time. And with any luck, responding to them would require him to make use of the many tomes on the bookcase in front of the desk. She made sure her own duties kept her in a position to intercept the girls and to hear any commotion from the library.

Unfortunately, the girls soon tired of painting. Sylvia hastily organized a visit to the sickroom, which seemed to please Ariadne if no one else. The girls complained of watercolor stains on their pale muslin dresses, but Sylvia ignored that as well. The conversation, which had never been interesting from Sylvia's point of view, quickly turned stale. Worse, playing nursemaid to them kept her from eavesdropping on the goings-on in the library. For all she knew, David had been crushed hours ago.

Sylvia was completely out of patience with the lot of them, so much so that she knew she was beginning to show it. She could not stop her comments from becoming snide, her glances scathing. Miss Alexander obviously recognized the signs as well, for the woman tried to suggest alternative divertissements. Sylvia welcomed the help at this point, even if it came from an unlikely ally. However, it wasn't until the art teacher mentioned reading aloud that she got any kind of response from the girls.

"Oh, Miss Alexander, I'm tired of the Good Book," Ariadne complained. "Can't we read Lord Byron's works again? His poetry is so romantic."

Personally, Sylvia found it incomprehensible drivel. But she was too pleased by the turn of conversation to intercede.

"No. Mrs. Radcliffe," Daphne insisted. "Her novels are so exciting!"

"I'd rather read Hannah Moore's work," Lady Emily maintained. "I like a heroine who suffers."

Hannah smiled, although Sylvia could not see anything in the conversation to please her. "I expect you have quite a number of choices at Brentfield," Hannah said. "Based on the other treasures we've seen, Lord Brentfield must have a wonderful library."

"It's tremendous," Priscilla bragged. "The shelves are eight feet tall and positively crammed with every book you could imagine."

Sylvia frowned at her. Did the girl want to be taken for a bluestocking?

"Not that I have time to read while I'm here, you understand," her niece hastily added, obviously catching the look.

This was Sylvia's opportunity. "His lordship is in the library right now," she put in sweetly. "I'm sure he wouldn't mind selecting a book for you. You might try that case near his desk."

They all brightened at this, although Miss Alexander took some pains to hide it. So, her warnings had not taken as deep a root as she had hoped. The woman still yearned for the sight of him. Time for more persuasive arguments later, if need be. With any luck, she would be sending Miss Alexander packing before the day was out. People in mourning hardly held house parties. Pity that she'd have to wear the black a while longer. Still, maybe Society would forgive her for not mourning overlong over David. It wasn't as if they were even related.

She carefully encouraged them, watching with satisfaction as they trooped from the room with promises to Ariadne to bring back something delightful. Sylvia made inane conversation with the girl until she was sure they must have descended the grand stair. Then she excused herself as well. She hurried to the landing and listened. Within moments, someone screamed and the mansion shook with the fall of a heavy object.

Sylvia smiled.

Thirteen

It had indeed been a long night for Hannah. Lady Brentfield's rather unpleasant conversation had only served to confirm what she had been fearing all along. Hannah had to make a choice. If it had only been a choice between her painting and the love of a wonderful man, she would have had no difficulty making her decision. Much as she loved her painting, she had no doubts that she would love David more. But what she feared was that the choice was between her happiness and that of David's.

He needed an aristocratic wife. That was clear to her, even if he had yet to fully realize it. He would find it hard to make his mark in English Society if all his peers perceived him as the rustic American Lady Brentfield did. Having a wife who was a penniless nobody would not help. If she married him, he might be shunned completely. She did not think that would help their marriage in the long run.

She could also not imagine living the life Lady Brentfield described. Managing servants? Entertaining all summer? Hunting? She had neither the interest nor the experience to do any of those things. She knew Lady Prestwick had been a countess and avoided such roles. Of course, Lady Prestwick was also viewed as a decided oddity. Would David be happy if Hannah wanted a more quiet life?

Then, of course, there was the matter of the line of succession. She had never really understood children. There were times when she could not remember being one. She supposed she must have been a quiet, dreamy-eyed child, not nearly as dark in soul as Lady Emily. Teaching at the Barnsley School had only confirmed her fears about her antipathy for young people. She had thought herself quite content in not having any of her own.

But surely David must have children. He had come all the way from America, at great sacrifice to his own hopes and dreams, to salvage this estate. He was the last of the Tenants. He had to have sons if the line was to continue. She was not sure she could give him those sons.

There was only one answer that she could see, and it broke her heart to realize it. If David asked her to marry him, she would have to refuse him, for his own good.

Her resolve, though painful, was easy to keep as long as she did not lay eyes on him. However, she found her heart beating faster as she approached the library with the girls.

"Perhaps we shouldn't interrupt him," she suggested, feeling craven, as Priscilla reached for the door handle.

"Aunt Sylvia said it was all right," Priscilla replied, never faltering for a moment. Hannah felt a twinge of annoyance that Lady Brentfield's needs should take precedence over David's, but she kept her mouth shut as the girl opened the door and they all peered inside.

Like everything else in Brentfield, the library was immense. It was long and narrow, with an oak-framed fire-place opposite the door. Except for the fireplace and north-facing wall, which held two slender windows, every space was filled from floor to ceiling with glass-fronted oak bookcases. Additional rotating book tables dotted the room. To the right of the door, surrounded on three sides by bookcases, a walnut desk crouched on clawed feet, its top littered with papers and additional books, most of which lay open. Behind the desk, unbending from his perusal of them, sat David.

He looked up and grinned at them, obviously glad for the interruption. As usual, his smile of welcome warmed as it reached Hannah, and she found herself blushing again.

"We have come for a book to read to Ariadne," Priscilla announced. "You're to pick one out for us."

Hannah frowned at the girl's presumption. "What Miss Tate means is that we were hoping you might make a recommendation."

Daphne gazed about her in wonder. "Please do. I wouldn't know where to start."

"Do you have any sermons?" Lady Emily wanted to know.

David stood and offered them a bow. "It would be my pleasure to pick out a book for you. Some of my personal favorites are in this case, in front of the desk where I can reach them when the estate business gets too boring." He paused to wink at them. "Which it usually does. There's even a Washington Irving I brought with me from America, *The Legend of Sleepy Hollow.* But it's not for the faint of heart."

"Sounds delightful," Lady Emily declared. "Fetch it for us, Daphne. You're the athletic one."

Daphne made a face, but David pointed to a shelf and she moved to comply. Hannah looked away from the girl to find herself facing David, who had left the desk to join her.

"How goes it?" he asked her quietly. "Is the painting class over so soon? I wanted to come watch."

Thankful for something to discuss, Hannah started to explain the girls' lack of interest. A movement caught her eye. Daphne had swung open the glass doors and was tugging at a book. What struck Hannah with horror was that the bookcase was leaning farther forward with each tug. David must have seen her look of fear, for he whirled, just as the oak mammoth began to topple. Hannah's body seemed to freeze as it veered toward her, but David shoved her out of the way. Then it was her heart that froze, as he raced forward to push Daphne to safety as well.

Priscilla screamed as the case came down. Glass shattered, sending shards in all directions. Books thudded to the floor. The oak frame hit the desk with a crash that sent a ripple through the wood at their feet. Hannah stumbled, clutching the case next to her for support. Lady Emily and Daphne hung onto each other and Priscilla collapsed into an armchair. Plaster from the exposed wall rained down, filling the air with gritty dust.

"David!" The cry burst unbidden from Hannah's lips. Her next breath filled her mouth with dust. She coughed, batting away the cloud to clear her vision. "David! Are you all right?"

He rose from the far side of the case, powdered a ghostly white by the plaster and rubbing his left elbow. "It's all right. I'm fine."

Hannah choked back a sob of relief as he made his way to her side. She hugged him to her. Some part of her brain informed her that this was not the proper reaction for a disinterested art teacher, but she refused to listen. "Thank God," she murmured against his dusty chest.

He stroked her hair. "I'm all right, Hannah. Don't be frightened." She felt him glance up and heard him raise his voice. "Is everyone else all right?"

Hannah collected herself with difficulty and raised her head, although she kept her arms firmly about him. Priscilla nodded in response to his question, wide-eyed. Lady Emily stared at the wreckage in fascination and Hannah, recognizing the look, knew she would shortly be seeing a painting to commemorate the event.

Daphne spoke up from her place of safety on the other

side of the fallen bookcase. "You saved my life, Lord Brentfield! That was amazing!"

"What's the word you Brits use?" David grinned. "Ah, yes, smashing." Hannah felt a nervous laugh bubble up at the absurd pun.

"Hardly the time for levity," Asheram declared from the doorway. "Is anyone hurt?"

"We seem to be fine," David assured him. He glanced down at Hannah, and she stared up at him, her body trembling. She knew she should move away, but she couldn't seem to release him. As Asheram picked his way through the rubble, David bent his head to hers.

"Much as I love holding you, sweetheart, you really have to let go. You should get out of here in case something else comes down."

Hannah swallowed, making herself lower her arms and step back. David chucked her under the chin and winked at her, forcing an answering smile from her. She willed her heartbeat to return to normal as he turned to motion Mr. Asheram to help her over the debris.

Lady Brentfield was waiting in the corridor as Hannah and Lady Emily were handed out. Other servants hurried from the kitchens.

"I heard the commotion from upstairs," her ladyship explained. "What's happened? Was anyone hurt?"

"We're fine," Hannah assured her, and was surprised to see a frown that could only be annoyance appear on the woman's face. Lady Brentfield had not struck her as an overly hospitable hostess, so her ladyship could not be worried about how this accident would affect the success of her house party. Before Hannah could wonder further, Daphne scrambled out of the room.

"A bookcase fell and nearly crushed me," she declared. "Lord Brentfield saved my life. He is a hero!"

The frown deepened. "But he wasn't hurt?"

Hannah peered closer. Was the woman truly worried

about David? Somehow, she would not have thought it of her. Lady Brentfield ignored her pointed look.

"No," Mr. Asheram answered for them as he helped Priscilla out as well. "His lordship is quite well."

"How . . . marvelous," Lady Brentfield remarked. To Hannah's mind, she looked anything but pleased. Then she glanced about at the girls. "Why, you're filthy. Haversham, see that baths are drawn for the girls immediately."

"Right after we clean up Armageddon," Mr. Asheram assured her, nodding to two of the footmen to come assist him. Hannah tightened her lips to keep from smiling.

David poked his head out of the doorway. "Go along, you all. Asheram and I will take care of this. How about we regroup in the blue room in an hour for lunch?"

"The Blue *Salon*," Lady Brentfield snapped. "And it will take us much longer to recover from this catastrophe. We will have lunch in our rooms and a nap to restore our sensibilities. I do not see how we can possibly join you until dinner."

David raised an eyebrow. "Very well, if you're sure." He glanced down at his own ruined apparel. "It will probably take me longer than an hour to clean up anyway, now that you mention it. Dinner it is."

Hannah did not argue as Lady Brentfield shepherded the girls upstairs. Indeed, her nerves were raw. He had nearly been killed! She said another prayer of thanksgiving that he had been spared. She could not think of a single classical reference for the moment. It was just as well. She knew if she had tried to draw at that moment, her trembling hands would have betrayed her.

She also knew she had a duty to perform before she could retire to the quiet of her room. She went first to Ariadne. As she had suspected, the girl had also heard the crash and was anxious to hear what had happened. Hannah gave her a sketchy account, promising to return after she herself had had a bath and changed.

Despite Lady Brentfield's assessment, it did not take Hannah longer than an hour to set herself to rights. Her hair unbound and falling past her thighs, she padded about the room in her dressing gown and bare feet. She had just resigned herself to wearing her other uniform when there was a knock at the door. Daphne bounded in on her response, Lady Emily and Priscilla trailing her.

They were still in their dressing gowns as well, although their gowns were satin to her flannel and dotted with laces and bows. Their hair curled in damp swirls about their faces. "We could not wait," Daphne announced, throwing herself down on Hannah's bed. "We simply had to talk to you about it."

"About what?" Hannah asked. She should have felt dismayed that they had sought her out. She wasn't entirely sure what to say to them when she wasn't teaching them about painting. Nonetheless, it encouraged her that they would voluntarily seek her out.

"About the ordeal through which we have all passed," Lady Emily intoned.

Priscilla shook her head, golden hair falling into natural waves about her shoulders. "They continue to go on and on about that silly accident in the library, Miss Alexander. Do tell them to stop being so childish."

"I'm not being childish," Daphne maintained. "It's perfectly natural to want to discuss something of great importance."

"Particularly when it involves life and death," Lady Emily agreed.

Hannah glanced at the two earnest faces and Priscilla's scornful smirk. "I suppose it is only natural to see how others might feel about the same event," Hannah allowed. "It helps us to put our own feelings in perspective."

"Exactly!" Daphne crowed, beaming.

Priscilla sniffed. "Well, I can tell you my feelings are not the least swayed by the entire affair. If you ask me, this house must have fallen into a shocking state of disrepair since the previous earl died, for something as sturdy as that bookcase to give way. When I'm mistress of Brentfield . . ." She stopped suddenly and looked away, biting her lip.

Hannah felt for the girl, who was clearly never going to be mistress of Brentfield. She patted Priscilla's shoulder. "When you marry and have a great house such as this, I'm sure you'll run it with style and elegance."

Priscilla smiled at her. "Yes, I shall. And my house parties will be the talk of the country. Everyone will want to visit me."

"I don't see why," Daphne grumbled. "One can only take so much bragging."

Priscilla's green eyes flashed. "Well, I like that. See if I ever take pity on you again, Daphne Courdebas. And I'll have you know that it isn't bragging when it's perfectly true!"

"Oh, stop it," Lady Emily snapped. "Nothing you've said has been true. You promised us sport, and until the bookcase came down I must say I've been bored nearly to distraction. You promised us stimulating conversation, and even though his lordship has an interesting sense of humor, all you've done is brag and belittle us. You promised us beautiful surroundings, and while the artworks are interesting, you are right that the house seems to need work. You promised us we'd see a betrothal before we left, and his lordship doesn't seem the least interested in you. In fact, I'd say he has developed quite a *tendre* for Miss Alexander."

"That's enough," Hannah declared, hoping to prevent a discussion of her own affairs and avoid the war that was brewing between the girls. To her surprise, Priscilla's haughty face melted into sorrow.

"You're right," she sniffed, tears pooling. "It's all perfectly horrid, and I know you all must hate me!"

"Certainly not," Hannah said, glancing at the other

girls sternly. Daphne instantly looked contrite; Lady Emily looked skeptical.

"Well," Lady Emily observed, "realization is the first step toward salvation. I daresay we don't hate you, Pris, but you could go a long way to making things more pleasant around here."

Priscilla sniffed again. "Yes, you're right. I'll try harder, really I will. It's amazing how a brush with death can change one."

"There, you see?" Daphne beamed. "We did need to discuss it. What are you going to wear to dinner tonight, Miss Alexander?"

Hannah hid a smile at their quick retreat into their normal concerns. What a shame adult difficulties were not resolved so easily.

"I'll be wearing my other uniform, of course," Hannah told them. They all looked disappointed.

"That will never do," Lady Emily declared. "While I enjoy the dark colors myself, when one is courting, one should try to look more festive. Bright colors attract the male."

Hannah choked on her laughter. "Girls, please! I'm not courting."

"Of course you are," Priscilla declared. "Even Aunt Sylvia has accepted that fact."

Hannah started to protest, but Daphne jumped off the bed and stalked to the wardrobe, throwing open the doors. "She's right," she announced. "There's nothing in here but her other uniform, some drab navy thing, and her painting smock."

"Which should have been expected for a teacher," Lady Emily confessed. "We shall simply have to take matters into our own hands."

"Now, girls," Hannah tried again, alarm rising.

Priscilla walked around her, eyeing her. "She's taller than either of you, and has a better figure than Ariadne. It will have to be one of my gowns."

"It will have to be no such thing," Hannah maintained heatedly. "Your aunt would never forgive me if I wore one of your dresses, Priscilla. Besides, I'm not a schoolroom miss. You cannot expect me to wear white."

"That lavender thing your great Aunt Myrtle sent you for Easter last year," Lady Emily replied as if Hannah had not uttered a word. "The one with the ruching about the hem, which you hated. It might do."

"It would not," Hannah protested. "Girls, this has gone far enough. I will not wear Priscilla's dress."

Priscilla smiled at her in commiseration. "I would hate to wear hand-me-downs too, Miss Alexander, truly I would. But beggars cannot be choosers. I think Lady Emily is quite right about the lavender dress. And Daphne has a set of amethysts that might suffice."

Daphne snapped her fingers. "The very things!"

"No," Hannah told them sternly. "No, no, and no."

Priscilla took her hands and looked at her beseechingly. "Oh, please, Miss Alexander? This is my first chance to do a good deed. You wouldn't want me to have a relapse into selfishness, would you?"

"Well, *I* certainly wouldn't," Daphne declared. "Do say yes, Miss Alexander."

"I should feel like a great big doll," Hannah told them, but glancing about at the entreating faces, she could see that nothing she could say would dissuade them. They all so badly needed a pleasant distraction after the dangers of the morning. While being dressed up might not amuse her, it would certainly amuse them. She sighed. "Oh, all right. Do what you can. Just remember, you cannot make a silk purse from a sow's ear. I have no expectations that anything will change just because you manage to gown me more suitably."

"You'll see," Priscilla promised, eyes shining. "We'll bring his lordship to propose, just you wait."

And that, Hannah reflected as they set to work, would be the very worst that could happen.

Fourteen

It was a beautiful dress. The silk flowed over her hand in ripples the color of spring lilacs, shimmering in the candlelight. The cap sleeves and the square-cut neck were edged in a darker purple satin, which also decorated the hem in a foot deep of swirled ruching, the puffy folds of similar material curling like grapevines. The necklace and ear bobs Daphne produced were a series of amethyst flowers, each center of black jet surrounding a single diamond. They glowed against Hannah's almond skin.

"Nearly perfect," Priscilla pronounced as Hannah stood before the pier glass mirror in the girl's bedchamber.

Hannah stared at herself, emotions warring. How wonderful it would be to wear something so lovely, something bright, something happy! Yet truth be told, she was wearing it as much for David's appreciation as her own. Somehow it seemed wrong to want to catch his eye when she had already resigned herself to refusing him. She glanced around at the three beaming faces and realized how much she would disappoint them if she cried off now. She forced a smile.

"It's beautiful," she agreed.

Satisfied, they allowed her to go visit Ariadne while they changed as well.

To Hannah's surprise, the girl was up and just finishing her own toilette. Though pale and a little thinner,

Ariadne appeared ready to return to her regular routine. Her enthusiastic endorsement of Hannah's attire made Hannah's spirits rise despite herself. When the other girls joined them, each of them in bright silk, they made a merry group going down to supper.

As they stepped into the Blue Salon, Hannah's stomach knotted. What if he didn't notice? Worse, what if he didn't approve? She instinctively sought him out against the windows and when she saw him, it was her own reaction she suddenly feared.

For whatever reason, David had finally decided to change out of his habitual tweed suit. Tonight he wore the black cutaway coat and breeches of a cultured gentleman. The white silk cravat, folded elegantly about his long neck, brought out the blue of his eyes. The cut of the coat and the tightness of the breeches made her acutely aware of how broad his shoulders were and how long his legs. When she had first encountered him, he had been David the Shepherd. Tonight, he was David the King.

The girls dropped curtsies around her, and when she continued to stare like someone demented, Priscilla tugged her down as well. *Have I learned nothing in three days?* Hannah thought as she lowered her gaze. *I still cannot seem to stop devouring him with my eyes!*

When she rose, it was to find David staring at her just as fixedly. The warmth of his gaze only served to discompose her further. She was not so far gone, however, that she failed to notice Daphne elbowing Lady Emily in the ribs, grinning in obvious pleasure at the response to their efforts.

"Ladies," he said in greeting, bowing low. "Thank you for joining me, and Miss Ariadne too! What a welcome surprise. We're just waiting for her ladyship before we can go in to dinner."

"Wait no longer," Lady Brentfield replied from behind

them. She stepped around them with a smile, which faded
as she caught sight of Hannah. Hannah stiffened.

"How lovely you all look this evening," she declared,
eyes narrowing. "That is a delightful dress, Miss Alexander. It puts me in mind of one in Priscilla's closet."

Hannah swallowed, guilt pouring over her anew. Lady
Brentfield had offered her niece the perfect opening,
and Hannah feared Priscilla's generous streak had not
lived long enough to endure such a blatant call for attention.

The girl surprised her. "Miss Alexander's is much pret-
tier," she replied, although she did accompany the remark with her customary toss of her head. "Besides,
purple makes me look bilious."

Lady Brentfield managed a smile. "Yes, it is a difficult
color to carry off. That's why it's generally reserved for
spinsters and dowagers."

"What a shame," David remarked, reaching out to
bring Hannah's suddenly cold fingers to his lips. "For it's
a lovely color, especially on Miss Alexander."

He kissed her fingertips, his warm breath heating her
skin inside the silk gloves. The girls stared, fascinated.
Hannah, knowing all eyes were on her, tried to remain
cool and composed, but she could not seem to keep herself from trembling at the sweetness of his touch. The
girls obviously noticed, for they exchanged looks of triumph. Lady Brentfield turned away.

Despite her ladyship's attitude, dinner was a merry
affair, and David retired with them immediately afterward to the Blue Salon rather than wait for his port
alone. Even Mr. Asheram joined them, taking his solitary
place beside the doors. Hannah smiled at him, and he
returned the smile with a kindly nod. Then he focused
on Lady Brentfield, and his look became decidedly less
friendly. Glancing at her ladyship, Hannah saw she had
seen the look and was glaring back. Hannah could only

hope that there would not be another conflict to spoil
the evening.

Priscilla hurried to the piano and set about playing a
waltz, casting insistent glances at Hannah while David
tapped his feet to the tune. Much as she would have
liked to feel his arms around her again, Hannah refused
to gratify them by providing further entertainment. Lady
Brentfield was angry enough as it was. She sat with her
back glued to the Hepplewhite chair, her slippers stuck
firmly to the Oriental carpet. After a time, Priscilla gave
up playing in disgust.

"After such a tiring day," Lady Brentfield remarked to
no one in particular, "I would think we should all retire
early."

This raised a chorus of protests from the girls, all, Hannah heard with surprise, directed at her.

"Oh, must we, Miss Alexander?" Ariadne pleaded. "I
feel as if I've been in that bed forever."

"I don't think it all that tiring a day," Daphne proclaimed. "I could stay up for hours!"

"In my family," Lady Emily announced, "we do not go
to bed until after midnight, even in the country."

"Well, I'm tired of playing," Priscilla pouted, at last
retreating to her usual self-absorbed attitude. Her friends
turned on her with quelling frowns.

"Well, I *am,*" she insisted. "Why don't one of you play
for a change?"

"Do you play, Miss Alexander?" Daphne urged, nodding her head in David's direction and winking boldly at
Hannah.

All eyes swiveled in her direction again. The only people who didn't look entreating were Lady Brentfield, who
glared, and David, who looked amused.

"Sorry," Hannah demurred. "I never learned."

"Poverty prevents one from learning so many of the
social graces," Lady Brentfield nodded complacently, sitting back in her seat. Hannah felt herself pale.

"Where are my manners?" David declared, rising. "You all have played and danced to entertain me. I should return the favor."

"Do you play, my lord?" Ariadne asked eagerly, even as Hannah blinked in surprise at his gesture.

"No," he replied regretfully. "But I have been told I have a reasonably fine singing voice. If someone would consent to accompany me, we'll put that theory to the test."

Priscilla hurried back to the piano bench, previous weariness obviously forgotten. "What shall I play, my lord?"

He looked thoughtful. "We'll have to think of something known on both sides of the ocean. Any ideas?"

"Do you know 'Greensleeves'?" Ariadne asked.

"No, not that," Daphne complained. "What about some native folk song?"

"I wouldn't know how to play that, silly," Priscilla scolded.

"We need something more meaningful," Lady Emily put in, and Hannah was sure she would suggest some funereal song. To her surprise, the girl had other ideas. "What about 'My Love Is like a Red, Red Rose'?"

David grinned at her. "One of my favorites. We've heard of the Bard of Scotland even in Boston. Robert Burns it is."

David and Priscilla put their heads together behind the piano. Hannah felt a spark of jealousy flare within her, and quickly put it out. The girl was getting attention for once for her talent. She had every right to enjoy it. Lady Brentfield evidently thought so as well, for she was watching the two of them closely. Hannah hoped she was not still harboring a desire to see the two of them wed, for David clearly had no such idea. Before Hannah could hope further, however, Priscilla played a run up the keys and David began to sing.

Hannah found herself staring once again. He had a clear, warm voice, higher than a traditional baritone but

not as high as a tenor. The words flowed gentle and sweet
from his lips and if she closed her eyes, she could imagine
that he sang them for her alone.

> O, my love is like a red, red rose,
> That's newly sprung in June:
> My love is like a melodie,
> That's sweetly play'd in tune.

> So fair thou art, my bonnie lass,
> So deep in love am I:
> And I will love thee still, my dear,
> Till a' the seas gang dry.

> Till a' the seas gang dry, my dear,
> And the rocks melt wi' the sun:
> And I will love thee still, my dear,
> While the sands of life shall run.

The message washed over her as gentle and welcome
as a warm bath on a cool winter night. She opened her
eyes, met his gaze, and realized he was singing the
words for her. The others in the room seemed to have
receded behind a gauze curtain. The only people in all
the immense great house were David and Hannah and
the only sounds were his tender voice and the beating
of her heart in time to a music only the two of them
could hear.

She didn't know how many verses he had sung, but
when he stopped, it was entirely too soon. The girls ap-
plauded wildly, even Priscilla on the bench. Asheram
added his acclaim from his station beside the door. Lady
Brentfield stifled a yawn.

David gave them a bow. "Ladies, you are too kind."

"Oh, sing another," Daphne begged, and the others

chimed in. Hannah wasn't sure which she feared most, that he would sing again and she would betray herself, or that he would not and she would never hear his sweet voice again.

Lady Brentfield stood, shaking out her skirts. "It was kind of you to humor the girls," she told David, "but I must insist that they get some rest. We have a busy day tomorrow."

"Doing what?" Lady Emily muttered. Hannah frowned at her.

Lady Brentfield must have heard the comment. "We are going into Wenwood to shop," she replied, eyes flashing as if she dared any of them to disagree with her. "There are some things I need in preparation for Easter, and I thought you all might enjoy accompanying me. Should you find anything that interests you, I will pay for it, of course."

Asheram frowned. Ariadne and Daphne brightened, though Lady Emily still looked skeptical. Priscilla's brow was furrowed, but she said nothing. Hannah wondered what was on the girl's mind. She somehow couldn't imagine Priscilla, even the reformed Priscilla, refusing a shopping trip.

"Just a little longer?" David wheedled with a wink at Hannah. He sounded for all the world like her younger brother when they were children, trying to get their mother to give up another cookie. Hannah would not have had the will to refuse him.

Lady Brentfield was obviously made of sterner stuff. "I try to keep the girls' best interests at heart," she sniffed, glancing pointedly at Hannah. Hannah felt a blush rising again. In truth, she would have gladly stayed up all night to be with David, a fact that only made her feel more guilty.

"I bow to the voice of wisdom," David replied, doing just that. "Good night, ladies, and pleasant dreams."

As he rose, he winked again at Hannah, and she felt

her blush deepening. Following the girls from the room, she reflected that once again she was unlikely to get much sleep that night.

Fifteen

David had never felt less like a gentleman as he wandered through the secret passage that night. Oh, he was still dressed in the clothes her ladyship had picked out for him when he had first arrived at Brentfield, but he had never felt that clothes made the man. No, it was his motives that made him feel like the selfish aristocrat he feared he was becoming.

He had spent the better part of a half hour after retiring arguing with himself, and for a person who prided himself on decisive action, that was considerable time indeed. Nothing he could say, no logic he could bring to bear, no moral lesson he could recite had been able to deter him from having his way. So now here he was, shouting his conscience into silence and doing as his heart bade him.

It was folly to seek her out like this, his conscience chided at him again as he carefully skirted a damaged portion of the passage. In the first place, no sincere man would take advantage of such a passage to reach his lady love unseen. In the second place, if they were caught, her reputation would be ruined. But he hadn't had a moment to speak to her today that wasn't surrounded by prying eyes. Besides, he itched to show her what he had discovered on his explorations of the night before when too he had been unable to sleep.

Ignoring the twinge of guilt, he held the candle high and hurried down the descending stair of the west wing, approaching the panel that opened to her room. There was a removable knothole, he knew, that would allow him to peer into the room before entering, but the idea of using it made him feel as if he were invading her privacy. Instead, he put his ear to the panel and listened intently for several minutes, just to be sure she was awake, alone, and properly gowned.

He thought for a moment she had company, for he could hear her talking. When no one answered, he realized she was talking to herself. No, talking was too mild a word for it. She was giving herself a downright scold.

"And what did you prove?" he heard her demand. "What did wearing that dress and jewels prove? You're still a nobody, Hannah Alexander. You can't play, you can't sing. Who wants a countess who paints? You can put on all the airs you like, but that isn't going to change the fact that you will never be his equal."

"Rubbish," David said aloud without thinking. On the other side of the wall, she gasped, and he cursed his ready tongue.

"Hannah," he murmured through the panel, "it's me, David. I'm sorry I frightened you. I had to see you. May I come in?"

She slid the panel away herself and stood facing him, hands on hips, cheeks blazing with obvious embarrassment. "How long have you been eavesdropping?"

"Only a moment," he assured her, stepping down into the room beside her. He wasn't sure whether to be relieved or disappointed that she had changed for bed. The shapeless blue flannel gown she wore hung heavy about her, obscuring her figure. He was surprised to feel himself stirring nonetheless. As she turned away from him to close the panel, he saw that her hair was unbound and flowing down her back like a river of molten chocolate. It was longer than he had thought, nearly reaching her knees, and it outlined her curves more effectively than the gown had done. He caught himself imagining what she would look like wearing nothing but the silken mass. It was then he realized that this visit was a serious mistake.

It was too late to escape, however, as she turned back to him, lips compressed. "You should not have used that passage," she scolded him, but he got the impression that she was still more angry with herself than with him. "This is unseemly. Do you know what will happen if we're caught? Do you want to be forced to marry me?"

The idea had never seemed more delightful, but somehow he didn't think that would reassure her. "No one is going to force anyone to do anything. This was too important to leave to a chance meeting, and from the sound of it, you won't be available tomorrow. Besides, I wanted to make sure you had gotten over your fright from this morning. You gave me a bad moment there in the library."

"*I* gave *you* a bad moment?" She frowned. "I'm not the one who was nearly crushed to death. And what was so important that you could not wait until daylight?"

"I found another passage."

She perked up, as he had hoped she would. "Really? Did you see where it leads?"

"I followed it far enough to know it goes quite a ways. I was hoping I could convince you to join me in exploring it."

"Now?" she replied, spreading her skirts. "In my nightclothes?" She seemed to suddenly realize that she was indeed in her nightclothes, for she hurried to draw the coverlet from the bed and drape it about her. In scant seconds, all he could see of her was the oval of her face, which was turning a becoming shade of red.

"Put on your wrapper," he said with a laugh. "Better yet, put on a cloak. I think the passage may lead outside."

She still looked skeptical. He put on his most pleading expression. "Please, Hannah? If I'm right, and this leads to old Lord Brentfield's art treasures, I'll need you to help me identify them."

She scowled at him from her mound of wrapping, then gave a mountainous movement that was probably a shrug. "Oh, very well. I must be crazy to humor you."

"No, just sensible," he replied thankfully as she waddled to the wardrobe to dig out her cloak. "Asheram says there's no arguing with me when I make up my mind."

"That's true enough," she agreed, throwing off the covers and masking herself in a voluminous brown cloak instead. He helped himself to a candle from her writing table and lit the taper from his own.

Returning to his side, she asked, "And is it Asheram? That's what you seem to call him. But Lady Brentfield and the servants call him Mr. Haversham."

"Her ladyship started calling him that, and many of the other servants have followed suit. I think he's given up correcting them. But his name is Honorius Asheram, and he's a descendant of the King of Ethiopia."

"Really?" she breathed as he opened the panel.

"So he tells me," he assured her, handing her the candle and helping her over the sill. He put a finger to his lips, mindful of the room on the other side of the passage, where Lady Emily lay sleeping. Then he held up the candle to light the way forward.

She had been a good sport to let him appropriate her like this, he thought as they climbed to the main passage and followed it to the intersection at the wing's corner. All the more reason for him to try to remember to behave. Still, he couldn't seem to keep from teasing her.

"Remember what I told you," he asked, deeming it safe to talk at last. "Which of these passages leads to my room?"

"That one," she replied, pointing to the correct passage. "But you needn't look so pleased as I have no intention of acting on that knowledge."

"You never know." He grinned. She put her head up

higher, and he set off down the north passage before she could argue with him.

"If you remember, I found the original passage because portions of the room didn't look right," he explained as they moved through the darkness. "I've wondered the same thing about the servants' stair. I checked it again last night and found another gallery leading off and sloping downward."

"Down?" she murmured, clearly as curious as he had hoped she might be. "But if it joins the servants' stair at the ground level, down could only mean . . ."

"Underground," he finished. "Exactly my thought. I'm guessing there's a room under the central courtyard, between the two wings."

They soon found he was right. The tunnel was well braced and wide enough for the two of them to walk side by side. While it was a little dusty, there was no sign of debris or decay. It crossed about half the distance between the west and east wings, perhaps half a city block. The tunnel ended at a wide, bronze-studded oak-plank door. It had an old-fashioned iron latch and a very large iron padlock.

"Well, how do you like that," David declared. "We come all this way only to be defeated."

Hannah was studying the lock. "This is new," she murmured. "It seems cleaner than the rest, and it's been oiled."

"Are you saying someone put it there recently?" David asked, lowering the candle and peering closer.

"Perhaps not as recently as in the last day or so, but certainly within the last year. I think, my lord, that you may indeed have found the location of the missing treasures. I cannot understand why the former Lord Brentfield would want to hide them away like this, but I think you should find out what is behind that door."

He nodded. "You can believe that I will." He winked

at her. "Come here with me tomorrow, and we'll both find out together."

"I wish I could," she sighed, with genuine regret he thought. "But Lady Brentfield will surely need my help. Believe me, I take no great pleasure in watching other people shop."

"You won't have to worry," David assured her, giving the lock a tug just in case. It did not so much as squeak. "Ash has been sending to Wells for anything we need. He tells me there are no shops in Wenwood."

"Does Lady Brentfield know that?" Hannah asked, clearly puzzled. "The girls are getting so bored. I think she is trying to divert them. Perhaps we should warn her ladyship that this shopping trip is doomed to failure."

"She must know Wenwood," he replied, more interested in how he might break the lock than in her ladyship's entertainments. "She's spent every summer in this house for the last five years, or so she claims." He shook his head. "Well, it's clear we'll get no farther tonight." He offered Hannah a bow. "Thank you for letting me waste your time, my dear Hannah. May I have the honor of escorting you home?"

She raised her eyebrows haughtily, but spoiled the effect with a giggle. "La, sir, you are too forward. Simply call my carriage, and I shall be off."

"Ah, but I insist," he said with a chuckle, holding out his arm.

"Then I must comply," she replied, giving him her hand.

She strolled down the passage at his side as if they were walking through the countryside on a brilliant spring day. David watched her profile from the corner of his eye. She was a quiet little thing, but game for adventure and not above a good tease herself. They fit together, like the well-worn strips of leather on an old harness—soft, supple, dependable. He found he would very much like that kind of dependence.

"Are you intent on being a painter then?" he asked casually, hoping she would not guess the reason for his questioning.

She started. "It has always been my dream." Her answer was as cautious as his question.

"You will not miss having a husband, children?" He wondered whether his questions would be seen as too forward, but he had to know.

She hung her head. "I fear I am not overly good with children, my lord. I wondered about that before I started teaching, but my current profession has only proven the fact."

He wanted to disagree with her, seeing how the girls had come to rely on her. But he sensed she was not in a mood to hear an argument. "Then painting will be your life. Will that be enough to fulfill you?"

"In truth, I had once hoped to have both a husband and my painting," she replied sadly, "but time has shown that most likely painting is all I shall ever have. That thought has not been overly troubling."

He waited for her to add "until recently," but she did not. Yet he seemed to hear it nonetheless. It was presumptuous of him to think that three days in his company would have changed all her dreams. He wanted to question her further, but they reached the servants' stair and conversation became more difficult, and more dangerous.

All too soon for David, they reached the crossroads. Although they could now speak with impunity, they also had reached the point where they would part.

Hannah dropped a curtsy. "I'll go from here, my lord. Thank you again for a memorable evening."

"You're welcome." Suddenly, he found the thought of leaving her untenable. "Are you sure you'll be all right?"

She smiled. "I'll be fine. I'm sorry I was so missish this morning. It's just that I realized how close you had come to getting killed."

"All in the line of duty," he joked.

"Don't," she murmured, reaching out to take his free hand. "If anything had happened to you, if I had lost you . . ." She broke off, snatching back her hand as if she realized she had said too much.

"Then you do care!" He wanted to crow his relief.

"What I feel is not important," she snapped. "You mustn't refine on it. When you enter Society, you'll find you have a host of choices, my lord. Any one of them would be better for you than I am."

"Rubbish," he replied. "I've had choices since I was fifteen. It didn't get me married, now did it? I've said it before and I'll say it again. When I marry it will be because I'm in love, not because I need money or an aristocratic wife."

She smiled sadly. "You're still thinking like David Tenant, not the Earl of Brentfield. You have an obligation to this estate, to the people on it. There are expectations about whom you can marry. An impoverished art teacher, or even a gifted painter, is not on the list."

"Hang their expectations," David swore. "And hang their list. They can dress me in fancy clothes, they can make me study papers until my eyes cross, they can even get me to hold a house party for girls fresh from the schoolroom. The woman I marry will be my own choice. And I choose you."

She gasped, and the candle shook in her grip. David took it away from her, blowing it out. A moment more and he had extinguished his own as well, laying the two candles against a beam in the utter darkness that followed.

"What are you doing?" she cried.

He pulled her into his embrace. "What I should have done the moment I met you." He lowered his head and kissed her.

She was stiff in his arms, but only for a moment. Then she melted against him, arms encircling his waist to pull him closer. The cloak parted, and he felt her curves pressing against his chest. She returned his kiss with a passion that set him on fire, her mouth warm and soft beneath his. He tightened his grip and deepened the kiss, lingering over her lips, then raining kisses across her cheek and down her neck. His hands tangled in the silken strands of her hair. She moaned, swaying on her feet, as if his touch left her weak.

He was suddenly glad for the darkness. He would not have wanted her to know how close he was to carrying her back to her room and making her his own. His desires must have been written across his face, and certainly other parts of his body were responding. He carefully set her upright, moving his hands to her shoulders. His breath was coming fast, and he swallowed before speaking.

"Hannah." His voice cracked and he shook his head. "Hannah," he tried again. "Do you understand? I'm in love with you, and I want you to marry me."

"I understand." Her voice trembled, and she gulped back what sounded suspiciously like a sob. "I love you too. Only don't ask me to say yes, not yet. We must talk, about many things. I don't know whether I can be a countess, David. I'm sorry to be so craven."

He gave a wry laugh. "You don't need to apologize. I've never thought I made a very good earl, although that hasn't stopped me from trying. As I told you, I keep moving until I hit a wall. Don't give me that wall, Hannah. Not after what we just shared."

"I don't want to. I need to think. Would you, would you please light the candle so I can go back to my chamber?"

He leaned over to retrieve the tapers. Pulling a flint from his waistcoat pocket, he struck it against the hardened beam. The candles sprang to life. She flinched away from the light, but not before he saw tears on her cheeks.

Guilt smote him. "Hannah, I . . ."

"No," she said, silencing him. "Not tonight. Know that

I love you and that I will do what is best, for both of us. Good night, David."

He watched until the glow of her candle faded in the distance. Then he made his lonely way back to the east wing.

Sixteen

Sylvia walked the corridors of Brentfield, still fully dressed, her black silk gown whispering to her of her failure. She had not been able to find the art treasures her late husband had left, which would have assured her future. She had not managed to attract David's attention or interest him in her niece, so she could not count on his support. She had not been able to keep him from courting that insipid art teacher, further damaging any chance she had of gaining a hold on him. And finally, she had not succeeded in bringing him to an untimely demise and ridding herself of him forever. It was enough to give anyone a case of the vapors!

There had to be a solution. Her next attempt on his life, calculated to occur while they were safely shopping tomorrow, did not strike her as being at all likely to succeed. It depended entirely too much on chance, and there was a strong likelihood that it would damage the house as well. Much as she longed for London, she had to own that a country seat had its uses, both as an occasional retreat and an exile for those who displeased her. True, she would only have it until the next fellow came to inherit, but she had every hope that that happenstance would be a very long time coming. She simply had to find another way to rid herself of David!

Her thoughts drifted back to the events of the evening.

David Tenant in formal wear had been most impressive
How well he would have looked on her arm, escortin
her about London Society. She had always thought h
would be a fine acquisition for a husband. She woul
have been the envy of every woman of the ton. Wh
should she have to give up so pleasant a dream for
sweet-faced spinster?

Which brought her back to what possible attractio
Hannah Alexander held for the man. She was pretty
Sylvia could be breathtaking. She was quiet; Sylvia wa
commanding. She was relentlessly kind and considerate
Sylvia knew when it was in her best interest to play th
termagant. She was so sweet as to be cloying; Sylvia wa
passionate and sultry. Besides, the woman had no ide
how to go about in Society, while Sylvia was an expert ir
deftly following and flaunting the rules. Why couldn'
David see that Sylvia was by far the better choice?

Her wanderings had brought her to the east wing, anc
it was only a few more steps to David's door. She pressec
her ear to the panel. She could hear nothing from within
Which would be easier, she wondered, explaining her de
sirability as a countess or smothering him with a pillow
while he slept? She turned the gilt handle and eased oper
the door.

The room was empty, just as before. A fire burned in
the grate, the bed had not been turned back, and the
candle beside the bed was missing. Sylvia frowned.

She glanced back down the corridor in the direction
she had come. She had seen or heard no sign of anyone
else awake in her ramblings. It was a large house, but i
had a single central corridor and so many rooms were
still closed. Only a handful were really habitable, and she
had passed them all without seeing him. Originally, she
had thought he was spending his nights with Miss Alexander, but she had never seen him tiptoeing in during
the night or out in the morning. And the schoolteacher
was quick to answer any knock from Sylvia, at virtually

any time of the day or night. So, if he was not with his love, where was the man?

A faint rustling came to her ears and before she could close the door, she saw a portion of the wall opposite her swing in on itself and slide open. She waited only long enough to be certain the person entering was David and that he was fully dressed before ducking back into the corridor.

She did not wait outside the door, but hurried away from his room. A secret passageway! Of course. Why hadn't she realized it before? Its existence explained any number of puzzles. Doubtless it led all the way to the west wing, perhaps to Miss Alexander's chamber itself. How, she could not imagine at the moment. It was enough to know that her suspicions had proven true. David had undoubtedly been using the passage to reach his lady love out of sight of prying eyes. She hadn't given him enough credit.

But perhaps the existence of the passage explained another mystery as well—the mystery of the vanishing art treasures. If Charles had known of the passage, he could have easily hidden the various paintings and sculptures along it, especially if he thought it would keep them from Sylvia's clutches. She still found it hard to believe he had caught on to her scheme; he had been so immersed in his hunting pursuits that she did not think he so much as noticed the rooms around him. Annoying man—if he could treat her so shabbily as to deprive her of a source of income he didn't even value, she was rather pleased that she had so neatly done away with him and his mewling weakling of a son as well. She should never have married into the family. They simply weren't good enough for her.

Sylvia smiled for the first time that evening as she strolled toward her own chambers. She could think of any number of uses for that passage. Tomorrow would indeed be an interesting day. She found herself quite looking forward to it.

Seventeen

Shopping in Wenwood was every bit as dreary as David had predicted. It failed entirely to keep Hannah's mind off the events in the passage the night before. In truth, she had slept little again. He loved her! Each time she thought of it she was filled with joy. The joy immediately turned to despair as she tried in vain to reason how she could make a good countess. She loved him in return, and she only wanted him to be happy. If only she could ensure that marrying her would provide that happiness.

She could not remember much about her parents' marriage. It seemed to her that her mother had been happy. Certainly she had seemed unhappy at her husband's early demise. Hannah remembered her mother often sitting in the sunlight of the window in the main room of their Banbury house, staring off across the country lane outside with a tender smile, as if she were remembering something sweet and long ago. She also remembered how her mother had encouraged her to accept the reverend's offer of marriage.

"He'll take good care of you, Hannah," her mother had explained. "And he won't mind that you paint."

Hannah had smiled. Sometimes it seemed to her that her mother saw her painting as some sort of handicap that must be explained, like having a relative who had once been sent to the Bethlehem asylum. "He's older than Father," Hannah had reminded her. "And he doesn't love me. Grandfather put him up to this."

Her mother hadn't denied the fact that Hannah's minister grandfather was trying to look out for his only granddaughter. "I'm sure the reverend will be kind and understanding. You'll have a roof over your head and someone to look out for you."

"Perhaps," Hannah had replied, "I prefer to look out for myself."

Now she wondered about the statement, said with so much pride and determination. She had made a way for herself through her teaching, and was on the verge of making an even finer way with her painting. Why did she suddenly long to give it all up for a man she could never make happy?

She forced the issue from her mind to deal with her task for the day. She was supposed to be the chaperone, and outside of seeing that the girls were in bed at a decent time each night and up again in the morning, she couldn't see that she had done all that much. Anyone would have reached out to Ariadne when the girl had been struck ill. Hannah resolved to spend more time with her charges until the trip was over. Part of her scolded herself for retreating from what was a far more important issue, but she told that part of her to be silent.

Although the town of Wenwood was only a few miles from Barnsley, Hannah had never had occasion to visit. All the teachers did their rare bits of shopping in Barnsley, or made an annual trip to Wells, and she could see why. The village of Wenwood consisted of a small country church with an oversized rectory and a cluster of laborers' cottages surrounding a small green. The largest cottage did have an extra room in the front with some dry goods, hardware, and fabric, but that was the extent of it. It was exactly as David had said. The only thing that surprised Hannah was that the owner of the cottage, a Mr. Delacorte, seemed to know her ladyship well. Hannah simply could not see Lady Brentfield shopping at the place.

"We'll pay the vicar a call," Lady Brentfield announced when the few bolts of fabric, all less expensive than the bright silk of the girls' morning dresses, had exhausted their dubious interest. The girls grumbled, but Hannah cast them looks of encouragement and they followed her ladyship down the dusty lane with ill-disguised boredom.

The Vicar Wellfordhouse was in the midst of teaching school, and was rather discomposed to find six lovely women standing in the doorway of what had once been the parlor of the rectory. Entrusting the care of the dozen or so children to his kind-faced female assistant, he hurried to greet them. He was a slight man, young for a vicar, she thought, of medium height. He had sandy hair and a bottle nose. His smile was gentle, and Hannah liked him on sight.

"Ladies, how nice of you to call," he assured them, although Hannah was certain it was a great inconvenience. "Lady Brentfield, isn't it?"

It did not surprise Hannah that her ladyship was not a recognized member of the man's congregation. It did seem to surprise Lady Brentfield that she was not more memorable. "It most certainly is," she quipped. "And with me are Lady Emily Southwell, the youngest daughter of the Duke of Emerson."

If Lady Emily noticed that the woman tended to wield her father's name like a sword, she did not show it. She nodded with just the right amount of condescension for one of her station addressing a mere country vicar. Reverend Wellfordhouse bowed over her hand with such care that she visibly thawed.

"And these are Miss Daphne and Miss Ariadne Courdebas, daughters of Viscount Rollings," Lady Brentfield continued.

Daphne dipped a wobbly curtsy; Ariadne propped her up. Reverend Wellfordhouse bowed over their hands as

well, setting them both to blushing. Hannah had to admire the man's fortitude.

"And, of course, my dear niece Priscilla Tate."

Priscilla batted her luxurious lashes at the vicar, who
blinked in surprise. He hurriedly covered the movement
with a bow.

"We are most fortunate to have them all visiting us at
Brentfield until Easter," Lady Brentfield explained as he
straightened at last. Hannah realized with a pang of annoyance that the woman did not intend to introduce her,
but decided it was one battle she did not need to fight.

As it turned out, the vicar fought it for her. "I hope
we can look forward to seeing you all at Easter services."
He nodded to the girls. Then he smiled at Hannah. "And
you must be Miss Alexander, the famous portrait painter."

Now it was Hannah's turn to blink in confusion even
as the girls beamed with pride that she was so well-known.
"Yes, how did you know?" she replied, trying not to notice Lady Brentfield's censorious frown.

"You are becoming quite famous in the area," he assured her with an honest admiration that brought a blush
to her cheeks. "I've had the good fortune to see the
painting you did of Lady Prestwick. And of course I had
heard about you from Squire Pentercast's wife. She is
quite looking forward to you painting their family when
you return from your visit to Brentfield."

"How is dear Genevieve?" Lady Brentfield interrupted
enthusiastically, managing to bring all the attention back
to her. This time, Hannah did not mind. She felt a little
guilty that the squire's lovely wife should be singing her
praises when she had had to delay the work of painting
the Pentercasts.

"Quite fine," Reverend Wellfordhouse replied cheerfully. "Young Allison is a year and a half now, and I understand from Mrs. Pentercast's sister that a little brother
or sister is due in October."

"Children can be such a blessing," Lady Brentfield replied dryly. The girls exchanged looks, and Hannah tried not to cringe at the sarcasm.

"Indeed." Reverend Wellfordhouse nodded. Hannah wondered at his wistful tone, but he continued in explanation. "I have always thought I would like children of my own. Of course, first I have to find a Mrs. Wellfordhouse."

He said it teasingly, reminding her of David, but the mere mention that he was still a bachelor propelled Priscilla, Daphne, and Ariadne into immediate flirtations. Hannah had never seen so many coy looks, batting lashes, and tossing curls in her life. Only Lady Emily remained aloof, and Hannah supposed that a country vicar, no matter how charming, was of little interest to the daughter of a duke. Within minutes, the poor man was red from embarrassment over the effusive attentions and Hannah was red from embarrassment watching her charges. Lady Brentfield apparently had had enough as well, for as the church bell rang two, she announced that it was time to return home.

The vicar politely bowed them out, but Hannah thought he looked relieved. She rather hoped they didn't stay for Easter services. She couldn't imagine trying to take communion with the girls simpering at him.

As the carriage rolled toward Brentfield, Hannah felt her spirits lift. In a few more minutes, she'd be seeing David again. Then she remembered how she had put him off last night. He had made his appreciation of her well-known. She would have to make a decision, and soon. If only she weren't so comfortable in his company; if only he weren't so clever and funny; if only he weren't so handsome; if only his kisses didn't make her yearn for more.

Her dilemma was still very much on her mind as the carriage came to a stop in front of the great house. However, the sight that met her eyes drove her current worries from her mind. Asheram limped out to greet them, clothes powdered in ash and smelling of acrid smoke.

"I regret to say, ladies, that there's been another mishap," he informed them as they leaned out the carriage window. "If you'll stay in the coach, I'll have you brought around to the side entrance."

Hannah grew cold in fear. "Lord Brentfield?" she begged, reaching out the open window to touch the man.

"Is fine," he assured her kindly. He glanced at Lady Brentfield, who was framed in the other window, and his mouth hardened. "Just fine."

"Thank God for small blessings," her ladyship quipped, leaning back inside the coach. Trembling, Hannah could only follow her lead and settle back as well. The girls raised a volley of questions, but she could only shake her head. It was all she could do to remain calm. Asheram had said he was fine, but until she saw him with her own eyes, she feared to find him injured as well. Several times she directed the girls' questions at Lady Brentfield, only to find the woman staring out the window of the coach, eyes narrowed in thought. Somehow, Hannah could not believe that she was also worried about David.

To Hannah's relief, David was waiting for them when they came through a little-used ballroom on the east side of the great house. This time she held herself back from running to him. Her heart leapt inside her, however, when she saw his clothes were as sooty as Asheram's and his right hand was bandaged.

"Well, ladies," he said to them with a bow, "this time you missed the excitement." He winked at Hannah, but she could see that his jovial response was strained. She managed a smile for his sake. "Seems someone left a candle burning without a holder and it eventually started a fire."

Hannah frowned, wondering about their adventure of the night before. Surely they had both taken their candles when they had parted.

"Clumsy servants," Lady Brentfield declared with a toss

of her head that reminded Hannah of Priscilla. "I would take the cost of repairs out of their wages."

"We don't pay that well," David informed her with bare civility. "I'm sorry to say that the blue room and the dining room have been damaged, as has the main entryway. The servants are currently setting up the upstairs sitting room in the west wing for your use. If you wouldn't mind having tea in the breakfast room, I'm sure it will be done by the time you finish."

As they murmured their agreement to his proposal, Hannah forced herself to take a deep breath. David did not appear seriously hurt, and none of the art treasures were in the rooms he had mentioned. They had indeed been fortunate.

"Lord Brentfield," Lady Emily intoned as they started down the corridor for the back stairs. "Where did the fire start?"

David glanced at her with a wry smile. "Ever the interest in disaster, Lady Emily?" he teased. "It started in the blue room, on the wall next to the library. I'll show it to you later if you'd like, but somehow I don't think everyone will be interested."

Hannah avoided his pointed look. In truth, just knowing he had been in danger was enough to set her trembling. She had no desire to see the location.

Lady Brentfield excused herself from tea and retired to her room, pleading a headache. Hannah would have loved to do the same, particularly as David excused himself to continue the restoration. She felt it her duty to see to the girls, however, so she played hostess and poured tea.

She had feared she would have to make conversation, but the girls were surprisingly quiet. It was Priscilla who requested that they also be allowed to retire to their rooms. Hannah had no choice but to retire as well, being unsure whether she could provide David with any help

in his efforts or whether she would only hinder his pro-
gress.

It was one of her few moments to herself since she had
arrived and she had no doubt how she intended to spend
it. She had ever thought better when she was drawing.
She hurried to the wardrobe and pulled out her sketchbook. Taking out a charcoal and sharpening it, she set
to work.

An hour later, she was beginning to feel as if she had
something. David's heavy-lidded eyes gazed back at her,
warm and inviting. She had captured his nose, she was
sure, but the mouth wasn't yet right. It was difficult to
capture that half smile he wore so often, the one that
made you think he was dreaming of something not quite
proper but sinfully delicious. It made her shiver just thinking about it. No, the drawing wasn't perfect, but even if
she didn't get a chance to do more with it, at least when
she left Brentfield she would have something more to
rely on than her memory.

There was a knock at her door, and the girls filed in
before she could call out to stop them. She snapped the
sketchbook shut and rose, putting on a smile. Four somber faces regarded her and she felt the smile fading.

"What is it?" she asked, her heart starting to beat faster
again. "Has something happened?"

They exchanged serious looks, which only served to
frighten her further. Priscilla stepped forward. "We have
something we must discuss with you, Miss Alexander."

"And you had better sit down," Daphne added, not
unkindly.

"I brought the smelling salts," Ariadne told her, pulling
the bottle from the pocket of her gown. "Just in case."

"Goodness," Hannah breathed, sinking back into the
armchair she had been using. "Are you giving me the
sack?"

"Are we allowed to fire her?" Daphne demanded of
her friends.

"I certainly wouldn't want to," Ariadne replied loyally.

"I daresay his lordship would be furious," Priscilla said with a giggle.

"Oh, you're scaring her out of her wits," Lady Emily complained. "Let me."

Hannah braced for the worst.

"Miss Alexander," Lady Emily proclaimed, staring her in the eye, "we think someone is trying to kill Lord Brentfield."

Hannah felt as if the ground were shifting beneath her. She must have paled, for Ariadne hurriedly thrust the smelling salts at her. Hannah waved the noxious smell away. "I know there have been accidents, of course," she acknowledged. "But murder?"

Daphne nodded vigorously. "I didn't want to believe it either, Miss Alexander, but Lady Emily can be most convincing. Tell her."

Lady Emily drew herself up to her full height. "It started with the poisoning. What did Ariadne eat that the rest of us didn't?"

Hannah raised her eyebrows. *"Did* Ariadne eat something we did not?"

Ariadne hung her head. "The strawberry tarts. I know Lady Brentfield told me not to, but they looked so luscious. I only nibbled on one, then took it and another up to my room for later."

"Perhaps they were spoiled," Hannah reasoned.

Ariadne shook her head. "The little I ate was quite fresh, I assure you."

"Quite fresh and quite deadly," Lady Emily intoned. "And meant for his lordship. They are his favorites, remember?"

Hannah swallowed, remembering.

"Then came the bookcase," she continued, hands clasped behind her. "The one case that contained his lordship's personal favorites, a case he used often, we were told."

"Only I used it first," Daphne admitted.

"Exactly!" cried Lady Emily. "We inadvertently foiled the murderer again. Now, today, this fire, smoldering out of sight, no doubt, right next to the library where his lordship would be working, where he might have been overcome by the smoke, choking, gasping, suffocating . . ."

"Please!" Hannah stopped her, her artist's imagination conjuring a picture that was more than she could bear. Ariadne obligingly offered the smelling salts again. Hannah shook her head.

"I told you she was convincing," Daphne bragged.

"But why?" Hannah cried. "And who? Who could possibly want Lord Brentfield dead?"

Lady Emily stood glaring at her for a moment more, then deflated. "I don't know," she admitted. "It gets rather fuzzy from here."

"None of us could think of a likely villain," Ariadne explained.

Hannah shook her head again. The tale seemed too far-fetched, a perfect melodrama for Lady Emily. The accidents were coincidental, but surely not homicidal.

"I appreciate your insights, girls," she assured them, "but I cannot credit that we have a murderer in our midst. Perhaps if this visit hadn't been so tempestuous—excitement one moment and boredom the next—you might see things from a different perspective."

Ariadne and Daphne looked thoughtful. Priscilla looked troubled. Lady Emily threw up her hands.

"I knew you wouldn't believe me. You wait and see, Miss Alexander. If I'm right, there'll be another attempt on Lord Brentfield's life tomorrow, and if we're not careful, this time it will be successful!"

Eighteen

As Asheram and David finished helping the servants put the damaged rooms to rights, they were having a similar conversation.

"Now do you see the truth of it?" Asheram demanded of David as they walked back toward the east wing. "Poisoning, crushing, burning. You're in danger."

David shook his head, feeling not a little weary from the day's exertions. He had hoped to spend the morning breaking open and examining the secret room, but Asheram had cornered him with questions regarding the estate. Feeling guilty for letting the older man handle so many of his affairs, affairs that only the earl should be forced to deal with, David had submitted to a lengthy discussion in the library. He was glad that the smell of smoke had alerted them to the fire before the flames could do too much damage. As it was, the restoration would take most of the day. The hidden room with all its secrets would simply have to wait. At the moment, all he wanted was a hot bath, dinner, and a moment alone with Hannah. He knew he would be lucky if he got the first two.

"I'll admit that these mishaps cut into my time to work on the estate," he conceded to Asheram, "but if you look beyond that, I'd say I've been lucky. My favorite suit needs cleaning and I singed my hand putting out the fire, but I didn't get sick, I wasn't seriously hurt by the bookcase falling, and nothing of any importance was burned. We should celebrate our good fortune."

"And hold your funeral tomorrow," Asheram grumbled. "At least let me post a footman outside your door."

"What good would that do?" David countered, stretching stiff muscles. "No one has tried to smother me in my sleep so far. And don't suggest I need a bodyguard or someone to taste my food. We're not talking about passing along the crown here. There isn't any heir but me."

"Do we know that?" his friend challenged as they reached the door to David's room. "What if someone else stands to gain? What if another Tenant descendant is lurking about the estate?"

"He has only to step forward and I'll give it to him," David replied, trying not to be heartened by the unlikely idea.

"But he won't know that. Perhaps he feels slighted that you were chosen instead of him."

"You should write melodramas," David quipped, pushing open the door. "Next you'll tell me this phantom long-lost cousin is hiding in the secret passageways."

"Well?" Asheram demanded, following him in to the room. "How do you know he isn't?"

Thinking of the locked door he had yet to open, David frowned. "I suppose it's possible, but not very likely. Still, perhaps we should take a few precautions."

Asheram smiled in triumph. David had a sudden vision of being followed everywhere by a phalanx of armed footmen. He'd never have another moment alone with Hannah.

"A *few* precautions," he repeated sternly. "I don't want our guests frightened."

"The first precaution," Asheram replied with equal severity, "should be to send our guests home."

"No," David told him. He strode to the wardrobe and began pulling off his soiled clothes.

He could feel Asheram frowning at him. "You're going to propose to her, aren't you?" he said accusingly.

David turned to grin at his friend. "I already did. She' a fine woman, Ash. I'd be proud to have her at my side.'

"Spoken like a Boston leather carver," Asheram ar gued. "Like it or not, you have to think like an earl."

He was tired enough that the refrain hit a nerve. "I you ask me, I'm thinking exactly like an earl. The aristo crats of my acquaintance are relentlessly self-centered anc selfish. I'll marry whom I please."

Asheram shook his head. "Very well. But what precau tions are you willing to take that you'll live long enough to see your wedding day?"

"Seal all entrances to the passageways we know about except the ones in my and Hannah's rooms."

"Of course," Asheram drawled.

David ignored the sarcasm. "Put the footmen to work as soon as they've recovered from today's excitement. We don't get many visitors out here, so we hardly need those strapping fellows at the front door. I want a constant pa trol through the house, day and night."

"Very good," Asheram agreed with a nod. "And I'l alert the household staff to watch for anything unusual. Thank you, David. You've set my mind at ease."

David grinned at him again before continuing to change. "With any luck, Ash, we'll both live to see my wedding day."

David would not have been so certain if he had known about the events that were to occur on the following morning. The evening had been spent in desultory con versation in the upstairs sitting room. Though it was a large room, the small, infrequent windows and crowded furniture made it feel cramped. Lady Brentfield was sul len; he supposed it was because of all the accidents spoil ing her visit with her niece. Priscilla was distant, and Lady

Emily regarded him so fixedly that he wondered whether he'd grown a third eye. Ariadne and Daphne could not maintain a conversation for long, and the frequent silence had become too lengthy to ignore.

Worst of all was Hannah's behavior. She was solicitous toward everyone but refused to acknowledge any of his teasing remarks. Indeed, whenever he so much as included her in the conversation, she would pale and look away. Most of the night she did not even meet his eyes. He had been at a loss to explain her behavior until he had asked about their visit to the village and been told about their reception by Reverend Wellfordhouse.

"He was quite charming," Ariadne enthused. "I'm sure he's a wonderful minister."

David had immediately liked the fellow when he had met him on his first tour of the estate. The fact that they both tended to take a stroll to clear their minds had made William Wellfordhouse even more welcome. In conversation, he had found William intelligent, well-spoken, and honest. "I've always enjoyed the good reverend's company," he told his guests. "I'm sure he equally enjoyed the company of such lovely young ladies."

Ariadne blushed, Daphne beamed, and Priscilla preened.

"Well, if you ask me," Lady Emily grumbled, "the only one he took any interest in was Miss Alexander. He went on and on about her painting. It was no wonder she was put to the blush."

"Isn't it entertaining how Miss Alexander manages to get all the attention?" Lady Brentfield quipped, sounding anything but entertained.

Hannah looked like she wanted to crawl into a hole.

So, William had had the audacity to flirt with her, had he? Why hadn't David noticed how utterly lacking the man was in social graces? He could not imagine what Hannah could see in him. William's eyes were entirely too close together, giving him a dishonest look. And what kind of minister let himself get distracted from his duties by a wealthy parishioner and four girls? David had gone to bed thinking that he should speak to Squire Pentercast, who held the patent for Mr. Wellfordhouse's living. Perhaps it was time they had a new minister in Wenwood. He was so furious he didn't even think to try the hidden room.

This morning he had wanted to shake himself for his unkind attitude. It had been jealousy, plain and simple. William Wellfordhouse was a good man, and David supposed he would even be considered handsome by the ladies. Certainly the unmarried young women of the parish thought so. Their antics after services each Sunday had been amusing as they vied for his attentions. David could see that the soft-spoken country vicar would be far more compatible with the gentle Hannah than the earl of a vast estate. She had said she didn't think she could be a countess. But the thought that Hannah might prefer the vicar's attentions to his own made him greener than the spring grass.

He was still struggling with himself as he walked to the breakfast room to join his guests. He found all the girls up, although Lady Brentfield had not appeared. Hannah slouched at the far end of the table, pale and strained. If that was a woman smitten, she'd be dead before her wedding day. Something was bothering her, and he did not think it was William Wellfordhouse. That it might be himself both reassured and troubled him. He had no opportunity to question or comfort her, however, for the girls set at him immediately.

"Will you spend the day with us, my lord?" Priscilla begged. "We've seen so little of you."

"The days are getting tiresome." Ariadne sighed. "It is enough to give one the megrims."

"I for one could use some exercise," Daphne put in.

"What has Lady Brentfield planned for you?" David

asked, hoping whatever it was would give him a chance for a moment alone with Hannah.

Lady Emily sighed deeply. "Nothing."

Hannah roused herself. "Lady Brentfield has not yet told us of her plans."

"She probably won't be up for hours," Priscilla complained.

Ariadne, Daphne, and Lady Emily returned their gazes expectantly to his. He stared blankly back at them. Then inspiration struck.

"Why don't you all go for a ride?" he asked.

As Ariadne, Daphne, and Priscilla perked up, Hannah slunk lower in her chair. David winked at her to assure her he meant her to stay home with him as before. Lady Emily's eyes narrowed.

"Will you be joining us this time, my lord?"

So, she obviously remembered how he had sent them off last time. He felt not the least guilty. "Sorry, Lady Emily," he explained. "I never learned to ride."

They were all properly shocked by his confession, except Hannah, who nodded in understanding.

"But you must learn," Priscilla told him. "All gentlemen ride. And you will be expected to lead the hunt."

"I have no interest in learning to hunt foxes or anything else," David replied kindly but, he hoped, firmly. "I'll be happy to see you off this morning, if you like, but I won't get on a horse. My own two legs serve to take me as far as I need to go."

His strength of purpose was apparently enough to deter further requests. They turned their attentions elsewhere.

"But you'll come with us, won't you, Miss Alexander?" Ariadne pleaded.

Hannah looked even less pleased by the idea than David had felt. "I know I should as your chaperone, girls, but I never learned to ride either."

"I simply do not know what the world is coming to," Priscilla complained with a shake of her tousled curls.

"An earl who doesn't ride? A woman who teaches impressionable young ladies and doesn't ride?"

"I don't teach riding," Hannah replied with some asperity.

"I have it!" Daphne cried, sitting straighter. "We'll teach them both!"

Now Hannah looked downright dismayed, and David knew exactly what she was feeling. The other girls chimed in with their enthusiastic endorsement of the plan. Before David could think of a graceful way out, Lady Brentfield wandered in. A quick glance at her showed him that she looked even more tired than Hannah, but she wasn't bothering to try to be pleasant.

"Lower your voices at once," she demanded, sinking onto the nearest chair. "You woke me from a sound sleep with all your chatter."

Ariadne and Daphne paled, exchanging glances. Lady Emily stiffened, mouth tightening. Hannah closed her eyes as if against a pounding headache. Priscilla bit her lip.

"Sorry, Aunt Sylvia," she murmured.

"What are you nattering on about anyway?" Lady Brentfield grumbled, glaring at the footman while he hastily brought her chocolate and cinnamon bread.

"Daphne conceived of a plot to teach Lord Brentfield and Miss Alexander to ride," Ariadne volunteered with a smile of pride at her sister, who blushed.

David waited for the explosion. Lady Brentfield found his refusal to ride more galling than nearly any of his other plebeian habits. She would surely not forgo an opportunity to complain, especially in her current mood. He saw Hannah grimace, and knew she expected it too. Lady Brentfield looked from one girl to the next. Her face broke into a beatific smile.

"Why, what a delightful idea! I'm surprised I didn't think of it myself. Hurry with your breakfast, girls. We shall start this very morning."

David stared at her, feeling the noose tighten. Hannah gasped as if she couldn't breathe.

"Your ladyship, I hate to be the one to stop an amusement," he started.

"Then don't," she finished airily. "You know you must learn, and you could not ask for more congenial teachers. Priscilla was practically born on horseback."

He ignored the vision her words conjured. "I'm sorry, ladies, but I must refuse. I would be a poor pupil. I don't even like horses."

"Surely you wouldn't disappoint your guests," Lady Brentfield pressed, making the act sound as bad as if he had stolen their virtue. The girls gazed at him imploringly.

"Yes, I would," he answered firmly. "I don't ride. I won't ride. Very likely I'll never ride. Thank you for your concern, ladies, but I must say no."

Their faces fell, but he refused to worry. He could not fall into the trap of trying to meet anyone's expectations but his own. Hannah was not so lucky.

"But we could still teach Miss Alexander," Daphne ventured. Her friends brightened. Lady Brentfield picked up her toast and examined it thoroughly.

"Yes, I suppose we could," she mused. "It won't be nearly as entertaining, but some good might come of it." She smiled a rather waspish smile at Hannah. "And you cannot cry off."

Hannah swallowed. "It's very kind of the girls to offer to teach me," she allowed, "but I have as much interest in learning as Lord Brentfield. It is not a skill I need."

"One never can tell," Lady Brentfield replied darkly, rising. "It is decided, then. Go change into your riding habits, girls."

"I don't even have a habit," Hannah protested, rising as well even as the color rose to her cheeks. Her fingers clenched the tablecloth. David rose too, intending to put a stop to what was obviously causing her distress.

"Priscilla can lend you one," Lady Brentfield replied with a wave of her hand. "Give her that brown velvet thing your mother picked out, Priscilla. She has the most abysmal taste."

"It will look lovely on you," Priscilla assured Hannah, before hurrying from the room. Ariadne and Daphne scampered after her. Lady Emily paused to eye her. David waited for Hannah to make her refusal.

"You needn't be afraid, Miss Alexander," Lady Emily told Hannah. "Riding can be rather pleasant. And you really should learn. My father would never let himself be painted by someone who was not versed in all the proper arts. I expect a number of gentlemen feel the same way. If you want to capture their attentions, you will have to prove you can live in their world. You don't want to be consigned to painting only women. They can be so petty." With an encouraging smile, she left.

"See you downstairs in an hour," Lady Brentfield warned, leaving as well.

Hannah stared at David at the opposite end of the table. One look in those deep brown eyes and guilt overwhelmed him. He strode over to her and took her cold hands in his.

"I'll tell them you refuse," he assured her.

She shook her head with a sigh. "No. The girls need something to divert their attentions, and I shouldn't anger Lady Brentfield any more than I already have. Besides, if riding makes me more appealing as a painter, then perhaps I should try. Horses are beautiful animals . . . to watch." She shuddered, then straightened resolutely. "Perhaps it won't be as bad as I think to actually ride one."

"Just to make sure, I'll come along," David promised her. She smiled gratefully up at him. The darkness of the morning vanished, and he bent to kiss her fingers. She slipped out of his grip and hurried away before he could do more.

An hour later, he stood with the ladies and Asheram in the courtyard outside the stables, eyeing a silver mare. The animal's eyes were as dark and gentle as Hannah's, but she seemed inordinately large to David.

"Are you sure she's a good choice?" he whispered to Asheram as Hannah approached the horse uneasily.

"She's docile enough to be a good training horse," his friend assured him, "but she has enough spring in her step to offer some interest. I don't think you'd want me to put Miss Alexander up on a slug."

"I think that's exactly what Miss Alexander would like," David argued, watching her stand stiffly beside the animal. He had to admit that Priscilla had been right—Hannah looked fetching in the deep brown velvet that hugged her curves and brought out the depths of her dark hair bound round her head in a coronet. Her face, however, was puckered with worry and David's heart went out to her.

"You must get to know the horse," Lady Brentfield instructed. She walked around the mare, inspecting it. She paused to pat its flanks and adjust its saddle. "Talk to it."

Hannah smiled wanly. "Nice horse," she ventured.

Ariadne and Daphne giggled. Priscilla nudged them to silence.

"Haversham, put her up," Lady Brentfield commanded, stepping away.

Hannah looked up at the saddle, just above her head. She stepped back. "I don't think I can do this."

David moved to her side to support her.

"Oh, don't be a ninny," Lady Brentfield snapped.

"So much for congenial teachers," David murmured to Hannah. Aloud, he ventured, "It does look rather high. How about if I hop up and check out the view first? Give me a hand, Ash."

"You don't have to do that," Hannah said quietly beside him. The grateful look she cast him strengthened his resolve.

"If it will make you easier, I don't mind," he assured her. He turned to his friend, who had stepped up at his call. "All right, Ash. Pretend I'm a beautiful woman like Miss Alexander and hand me up into that contraption."

"I haven't that vivid an imagination, my lord," Asheram quipped, but he cupped his hands and David set his foot to push himself up backward into the sidesaddle.

His first thought was that he wasn't sure where his left leg was supposed to go. His second was that the horse did seem ridiculously high. Hannah's worried face was at his knee. He had no time to settle himself or think of anything further, however, as the world suddenly exploded around him. The docile but spirited mare heaved upward, throwing him back against the saddle. He snatched at the pommel to steady himself, but she pitched forward, and he pitched headlong out of the saddle. The paving stones of the courtyard loomed up, and he knew no more.

Nineteen

Sylvia wanted to cheer in triumph as David's form lay still on the ground. She could not believe that her trap for Miss Alexander had actually netted her the earl himself. The only thing that could be more perfect would be if the silly horse actually stepped on him, completing its work. Her luck did not hold, however, as the horse dashed off like a crazed thing and several of the grooms hurried after it. Haversham hastened to his master's aid. Sylvia followed him, only to find the art teacher there before her.

"Is he?" she gasped as Haversham knelt at David's side.

"He's alive," the man confirmed, gently rolling him onto his back.

Sylvia sighed inwardly. Nothing was as easy as she had hoped. Still, he was helpless and in her power at last. The left side of his face was streaming blood and it seemed to her that his head was dented. That was something for which to be grateful.

Hannah sank down beside him. "David, oh, David," she murmured, reaching out to touch his pale cheek. "What have I done?" She used the train of her borrowed riding habit to stop the flow of blood. If Sylvia hadn't thought the outfit hideous, she would have taken her to task for soiling good velvet.

"What have you done indeed?" Sylvia demanded,

choosing instead to play the outraged matron. "If it wasn't for your selfishness, this would never have happened."

Hannah reeled as if she had been struck. Sylvia hid her glee, turning instead to the other servants who had come running at the cries of alarm. "Don't just stand there. Your master is injured. Take him to his chambers at once."

"Wait," Haversham ordered, glaring up at her. "We need to determine the extent of his injuries before we move him, or we might do further damage."

Sylvia cheerfully returned him look for look. He was David's trained dog. Without his master to guide him, he was nothing.

"We cannot wait," she argued. "We must get him indoors and send for the doctor." She pointed to a waiting footman. "You there. See that Dr. Praxton is brought at once. Until then, you three carry his lordship into the house."

"You aren't the one to give orders," Haversham growled.

"You dare to defy me?" She laughed, feeling power surge through her. She was aware of Miss Alexander's horrified gasp, and the girls stepping away from her, but she hardly cared. "I am the mistress of Brentfield. The servants will do as I say, if they know what's good for them."

She expected the man to argue, but to her surprise, the art teacher stepped between them. Her look was so furious that Sylvia was forced to retreat a step. "Stop it, both of you! We should be thinking of David!"

Haversham took a deep breath even as Sylvia blinked at the vehemence. The woman had teeth after all. What a pity it was too late to use them to any advantage.

"You're right, Miss Alexander," he murmured, bending over his master again. Sylvia held her breath as he gently wiped away the pooling blood with a handkerchief. Then he tapped David's cheek, calling his name. She felt her power surge again as David did not so much as move or open his eyes. Even a dribble of water from a cup a helpful groom offered failed to rouse him. Surely his life was draining by the moment. She had only to wait out the night.

"Well? Can we move him now?" she demanded as Miss Alexander began to cry silently.

Haversham did not acknowledge her. "Weimers, help me carry him," he ordered a young footman standing nearby.

It was only as they carried his limp body past her that she noticed the girls. Ariadne and Daphne were stunned to silence, and she was dismayed to see tears, of all things, in Priscilla's eyes, along with a look that appeared faintly accusatory. Lady Emily, however, was staring at her with a decidedly narrow look. Sylvia would almost have thought that the young lady knew what had just happened. Before she could think what she should do about the matter, Hannah stumbled past her in the wake of David's body. Sylvia caught her arm to prevent her from following them.

"I will see to his lordship," she informed the annoying woman. "Your place is with the girls. You are the chaperone. It's time you started playing the role."

Hannah blinked, clearly dazed, and Sylvia wondered whether she'd be of any use whatsoever. Any woman who let herself get so involved with a paramour that she became overset was not worth Sylvia's time. She pushed Hannah toward the motionless girls. "Go on. Do your duty. I must do mine." Hoping that the woman would at least stay out of her way, she hurried after Haversham. If David's injuries were serious, she wanted to be there when he succumbed. If they weren't, she would help them become so. One way or the other, David Tenant would not live to see another morning.

Twenty

Hannah's mind refused to focus on anything but David. His still body, his face so pale beneath the blood, seemed to be engraved on her memory. Painting after painting flashed before her, each more heartbreaking than the last—*The Fall of Icarus, The Death of Arthur, The Burial of Christ*. Only the last offered any hope; it was Good Friday after all. As her grandfather had taught her, another good man had been terribly hurt on that day and rose again. But no matter how she tried, she seemed incapable of believing that David would triumph.

That such destruction could happen in a blink of an eye terrified her. One minute he'd been smiling confidently down at her; the next he had been stretched unmoving upon the ground. For all she knew, his life had been taken in that moment. And Lady Brentfield had said it was her fault. This terrible accident was entirely Hannah's fault. She had not caused the animal to rear up like that, but it was her fault all the same. She had been doing anything to avoid having to face David regarding his proposal—not even trying to help with the restoration after the fire, ignoring his attempts at conversation last night, even allowing the girls to convince her to try riding for fear she'd have to stay behind with him if she didn't accompany them. If she had been willing to stand her ground and refuse to ride, he would never have gotten on that horse. Her own fears and inability to make a decision had destroyed him. She buried her face in her hands and sobbed.

She wasn't sure how long she had been crying when a voice penetrated the fog of her misery. "Miss Alexander?" Ariadne murmured. "What should we do?"

Hannah took a deep shuddering breath and looked up. Four worried faces confronted her. Ariadne and Daphne had tears running down their faces, and Lady Emily's lower lip trembled. Priscilla was so pale that Hannah thought she might faint. Until that moment, she had never realized how young her charges were. Ariadne still had not shed the last of her baby fat. Daphne's eyes were perpetually wide in wonder. Priscilla still dreamed of marrying a prince. Even Lady Emily, for all her dire predictions, sometimes showed a need for support from the others. Hannah held out her arms, and they crowded against her.

"It was awful!" Daphne sobbed. "I've fallen from a horse any number of times, but I've never been so still! He must have been so terribly hurt. Poor Lord Brentfield!"

"Head injuries can be very dangerous," Ariadne sniffed, her own head against Hannah's shoulder. "I hope Lady Brentfield knows to watch him closely."

"She'll watch him closely," Lady Emily predicted. "If you ask me, she is our villain."

Hannah gasped, and Priscilla broke away, eyes wide in her pale face.

"How dare you, Emily Southwell! I don't care if you are the daughter of a duke. You have no right to make such accusations. Aunt Sylvia would never . . . she couldn't . . . oh, Lord, what if she did?" She crammed her fists against her mouth and ran for the house.

Hannah could not move to follow her, with the others so close.

"Could Lady Brentfield be a murderess?" Ariadne murmured in apparent fear.

Hannah's arms closed around the girl in a fierce hug.

"I don't know. I wouldn't want to think such a horrible thing about anyone."

Lady Emily looked abashed.

"What should we do?" Ariadne asked again.

What should they do indeed? Hannah wanted nothing more than to run to David's side. But the girls needed her, and she knew staying with them was the right thing to do. Besides, if there was some sort of plot to these accidents, she could hardly leave the girls untended with the criminal on the loose. Hannah stiffened and the girls stepped back.

"The first thing we do," she declared, "is find Priscilla. And we will ask the servants to fetch us as soon as there is news of Lord Brentfield's condition." Her fears assailed her anew. He would be fine. He had to be fine. Her heart wouldn't survive without him. "And then," she added, "I think it would do us all good to pray."

David floated in a black sea of pain. It seemed he could see a faint glow in the distance, like a lighthouse on the edge of a dark sea or a candle at the end of one of his passages. Instinctively, he knew he should move toward it, but doing so only increased the pain. He relaxed instead, resting in the nothingness.

But something nagged at him. There was something he hadn't done, something urgent. He tried to think what it could be, and the pain intensified again. Annoyed, he fought against it this time.

He had been on horseback. Now why had he done a foolish thing like that? He'd never trusted the flighty animals. And he'd always thought it a waste of good leather to use it to decorate a saddle that was only going to cradle someone's behind. What could possibly have made him change his mind and get on a horse?

The pain tightened around his head like a vise and he gasped. Then he gritted his teeth, refusing to let it defeat him. He'd gotten on that horse to impress someone—no, to encourage someone. Someone who was important to him. Someone he'd give his life for. Someone he loved.

"Hannah!"

His eyes snapped open and light pierced them. He had momentary glimpse of Asheram's startled face before the darkness closed in again.

Finding Priscilla was not as difficult as Hannah had feared. The girl was facedown on her bed, thoroughly soaking the rose satin comforter with her tears.

"Ineffectual," Lady Emily proclaimed. "If you are truly repentant, we should see it in your actions."

"I don't think this has anything to do with repentance," Hannah replied, seating herself beside the distraught girl. "And I don't think it would hurt if you apologized."

"Neither my station nor the situation requires it," Lady Emily argued. When Hannah raised an eyebrow, the girl wilted. "Oh, very well. I'm sorry, Pris. But your aunt is the most likely suspect."

Priscilla shuddered and sat up. Hannah offered her an encouraging smile. "I know." Priscilla sniffed. "She has the temperament for it, I think. I've been wondering about her ever since you first mentioned that the accidents might be attempts on Lord Brentfield's life. But to truly believe she would be capable of murder? It's horrible!"

"Horrible and unfounded," Hannah insisted. "Lady Brentfield has not turned out to be the kind of hostess we had expected, but to go from disinterest to murder is a very long road. I think we should curtail these discussions until we have proof."

"We do have proof," Priscilla said quietly.

Hannah stared at her, feeling the blood drain from her face. "What?" she whispered.

Daphne, Ariadne, and Lady Emily crowded forward eagerly. Priscilla hung her head.

"Father told me that Aunt Sylvia was left out of her late husband's will. We don't know why. She'd only been married to the previous Lord Brentfield for five years, so it may be that he simply hadn't taken the time to revise the will."

"It's also possible," Lady Emily put in darkly, "that he recognized her true nature and refused to leave her anything."

Priscilla sighed. "Yes, that's possible too. Either way, she is beholden to the current earl for her living."

"But surely Da . . . the current Lord Brentfield will provide for her," Hannah protested, finding it impossible to believe that anyone she knew could be so wicked. "He's let her live in the great house. She's entertaining guests as if the place were her own. She should be grateful!"

"When have you seen Aunt Sylvia grateful for anything?" Priscilla grimaced. "She would see such gifts as crumbs and want the whole cake. She tried to marry him, you know."

"But she wanted him for you!" Hannah argued.

"Only after she found he wasn't interested in her. Then she decided to let me have a go at it. We tried to compromise him the other night."

"Oh, Priscilla!" Daphne cried as the other girls gasped and Hannah shook with mortification. She was supposed to be their chaperone! How could she have let them down, and David too!

Priscilla raised her head, pouting. "We didn't succeed. He wasn't in his room. Aunt Sylvia thought he must have been with Miss Alexander."

They were staring at her now. Could it have been the night she and David had gone exploring? No, Priscilla had already started helping her court him. Surely the girl would not have done so if she were planning on catching him for herself. It had probably been the night he had first found the new passage. She was grateful he had been unable to sleep.

"He wasn't," she assured the girls.

They nodded, apparently willing to accept her word for it.

"So," Lady Emily put in, "when neither of you were successful, Lady Brentfield turned to murder."

"Yes, I fear so," Priscilla sighed, lower lip trembling.

"I can't believe it," Hannah maintained. "Murder? Simply to have more than she needs?"

"Most assuredly," Lady Emily intoned.

"But if there was no mention of her in the will," Hannah persisted, "what would she gain?"

Lady Emily opened her mouth to respond, then snapped it shut again. She glared at Priscilla.

"Well, don't look at me," Priscilla said. "I'd be happy to find she's innocent. But I don't think she is. She's been doing too many strange things lately. She took us to visit the Earl of Prestwick when she loathes the man and everyone knows he refuses to marry so he isn't even interesting. She took us shopping in Wenwood when everyone knows there are no shops there. And she's the one who taught me that trick with the horse."

"What trick?" Hannah demanded, and the girls echoed her words.

Priscilla shrugged, picking at the bedclothes. "It's an easy way to rid yourself of a rival, only of course you don't expect that they'll actually be injured. Most young ladies of the ton know how to sit on a rearing horse. You only make them appear foolish. Only Lord Brentfield, of course, didn't know how to ride."

"But what did she do?" Lady Emily urged.

"You simply place a burr under the edge of the saddle. No one notices until the rider sits down."

"And the prickles are driven into the horse by the weight," Lady Emily concluded. "Of course!"

"She didn't seem the type to get to know a horse first to me," Daphne agreed. "Talk to the horse indeed." Hannah blushed, remembering.

"Oh, poor Lord Brentfield!" Ariadne moaned.

Lady Emily started. "No, not poor Lord Brentfield. Poor Miss Alexander! That trap was meant for her!"

Hannah started. "What do you mean?"

"Lady Brentfield could not have known his lordship would be so gallant. She put that burr under the saddle for you, Miss Alexander. She meant for you to be thrown."

Hannah closed her eyes. It all made an evil kind of sense. The girls might not be able to determine a motive for the woman's deadly acts, but Hannah could. Suddenly she knew why old Lord Brentfield had hidden his treasures and what Lady Brentfield had hoped to gain by David's death. With David out of the way, Lady Brentfield would have the run of the house. She could find the missing treasures and sell them. She could be living in high style on the Continent before the next heir, or the Crown, arrived to take ownership. Hannah could not imagine how her own death might benefit the woman, but perhaps spite was enough of a motive if one were prone to commit murder. She opened her eyes and found the girls staring at her again.

"You are right, I fear," she told them. "Lady Brentfield appears to be guilty."

"I knew it!" Lady Emily crowed.

Priscilla compressed her lips in an obvious attempt to keep from crying. Ariadne and Daphne exchanged glances.

"What do we do now?" Daphne wanted to know.

"Now," Hannah replied with determination born of love and fear, "we make sure she doesn't get a chance to finish her work."

* * *

The girls followed her willingly to the east wing, but getting any farther proved difficult.

"Sorry, ladies, but his lordship can't have visitors," the young footman told them. He had obviously been set on duty outside the bedchamber, but whether by Asheram or Lady Brentfield, Hannah was afraid to learn.

"Fetch us Mr. Haversham, then," Lady Emily demanded in her most ducal tones.

The footman moved to comply, but Hannah caught his arm. "Is Lady Brentfield in the room as well?"

"Yes, miss," he replied, clearly puzzled by their intensity. "She and Mr. Haversham are awaiting the doctor."

Hannah exchanged looks with the girls and knew they realized the danger of removing Asheram and leaving Lady Brentfield alone with David.

"Then we will wait as well," Hannah told the footman. "Is there a sitting room nearby?"

He pointed to a room down the corridor, and Hannah nodded. "Please let us know the moment the doctor arrives." She led the girls away from the door.

"Why don't we go tell Mr. Haversham?" Daphne demanded as they found seats in the wide room. "We don't have to call him out, we could go in to him."

Hannah shook her head. "Who knows what she'll do if we force her hand. I want her well away from David before we expose her."

Too late she realized she had used his given name. They giggled. The humor relaxed the tension in the room, and she was pleased to find that they passed the next while in almost normal conversation. The room was warm and pleasant, done in tones of russet and gold. She noticed that several of the paintings on the walls seemed to be the wrong color, and one of the walls was brighter than the others, as if some tapestry had been removed recently. Her lips tightened as she realized she was again seeing evidence of the attempted art thefts. Lady Brentfield was intent on robbing David, and future generations, of treasures meant to be shared. If only the woman could be stopped before she hurt anyone or anything else!

Twenty-one

Hannah encouraged the girls to say a prayer for David's recovery, but they had not finished before Asheram appeared in the doorway to the sitting room. He looked tired, but not devastated, which could only mean that David was still alive. Hannah jumped to her feet and ran to him.

"What are you doing here!" she demanded, ready to shove him back to David's side if needed.

The girls had leapt to their feet as well, and Asheram's eyes widened at their militant stances.

"You didn't leave Lord Brentfield alone with her?" Daphne accused.

"Return to your post at once!" Lady Emily demanded.

"Ladies, please!" He held up his hands as if in surrender. "I am not neglecting my duties, I assure you. I left Lord Brentfield in the fine care of Dr. Praxton."

Their anger melted. Hannah took a deep breath and forced herself to relax.

"How is Lord Brentfield?" Ariadne asked.

"Dr. Praxton feels there is reason to hope. Aside from the scrapes on his face, his lordship's external injuries appear to be minor."

Hannah let out her breath. "Is he awake?" she asked hopefully.

"Not yet. That is the one area of concern. The longer

he remains unconscious, the more likely there are internal injuries. Dr. Praxton says he must be monitored until he awakens. We thought he was coming around for a moment, but he lapsed back into unconsciousness." He paused, eyeing Hannah. "He spoke your name, Miss Alexander."

Her heart leaped, and she clasped her hands tightly together to keep them from shaking. Again she fought the desire to run to his side. First she had to tell Asheram of their fears about Lady Brentfield.

He listened patiently while she explained, the girls chiming in to reinforce or clarify the information. When she finished, his face was tight with obvious anger.

"I suspected as much," he told them. "Unfortunately, we have no proof. Lady Brentfield is influential in Society. We cannot simply accuse her and expect anyone to take us seriously. But don't worry. I promise she won't get near David again without someone there to stop her."

Hannah put her hand on his arm. "You do not know how long you will have to hold vigil. The servants fear her, so you cannot leave the work to them. Let me help you."

"Let us all help you!" Priscilla insisted, and her friends chorused their willingness as well.

Asheram shook his head. "I appreciate the offer, ladies, but I must think of your safety. As you noted, she has already lashed out at Miss Alexander. I cannot take the chance that she might attack you as well."

"Surely she would not attack me," Priscilla protested.

"Surely you would not want to be in a position to find out," Hannah countered. "I agree with Mr. Asheram. The four of you should remain as far out of this as possible." She turned back to the steward. "Mr. Asheram, may I have a word with you—alone?"

Priscilla stuck her nose in the air and flounced to the other side of the room. With an apologetic smile at Hannah, Ariadne and Daphne moved to join her. Lady Emily squeezed Hannah's hand.

"Be careful," she murmured before going to her friends. Asheram eyed Hannah expectantly.

"You must know I would do anything for him," Hannah told him. "I feel as if I failed him. Please, won't you let me help you keep watch?"

His face softened. "Miss Alexander, I understand your worries. I'm afraid they are blinding you to the circumstances. You are neither related to Lord Brentfield nor his servant. You should not be left alone with him in his bedchamber."

"These are hardly normal circumstances," Hannah protested. "Surely no one would judge me for caring for an injured man!"

"Lady Brentfield would judge you. And she would see that your reputation would be ruined. You could lose your post, your commissions."

"I don't care!" Hannah cried, then bit her lip as the girls glanced at her. She swallowed before continuing with a lowered voice. "None of that matters, Asheram. What matters is that David recovers. Her ladyship will leave the room eventually. Let me watch when she's asleep."

"If you're seen . . ." he began.

"I won't be," she promised. "I'll come and go through the secret passage."

He narrowed his eyes. "It just might work. Truth be told, I wasn't sure I could stay awake longer than she could. I'll send someone to fetch you when she leaves for the night. You're right—I can't see her ladyship inconveniencing herself, even to finish her nasty job. You'll see to the girls until they retire?"

Hannah nodded. "They'll be safe with me."

And so it was settled. The girls kept at her for a time, but she maintained a severity that ultimately defeated them. This time she did not vacillate. For once, she had no doubts as to how a chaperone, or a teacher, should act.

It was a long afternoon, but somehow they made it to dinner and through dinner to bedtime. By the time she had made sure each of the girls was in bed, there was still no change in David's condition. Dr. Praxton had visited again before retiring to his own home. He had confirmed David's unconscious state. All they could do was wait.

Hannah knew she should rest so that she could take Asheram's place later, but when she lay fully clothed on the bed, sleep refused to come. She tried praying again, but after a while she realized she was repeating the same pleas over and over and stopped. God had surely heard her and would respond as He saw fit. Belaboring the issue wasn't helping anyone.

She thought about drawing and went to fetch her sketchbook. One look at the half-finished picture of David, however, and she found she could not put charcoal to paper. His eyes gazed back at her lovingly. She ran her hand down his cheek. A tear threatened and she snapped the book shut before the drawing could be damaged.

A tap on the door jerked her upright, and she realized she had fallen asleep in the chair. The maid Clare poked her head in. "Mr. Haversham wanted you to know that Lady Brentfield has retired."

Hannah thanked her for her trouble. The minute the maid closed the door, Hannah was moving toward the secret passage. Opening the panel, she took the already lit candle from the writing table and stepped inside the passage. She climbed the stair carefully, thinking of the fire only a few days ago. When she reached the corner, she took a deep breath and plunged down the eastern corridor.

Darkness wrapped around her, her candle a tiny circle of light. Funny that she had never noticed how deathly silent the passages could be. When she had been with

David, he had been teasing or explaining and she had seldom felt afraid. Now she began to hear other noises in the darkness, furtive rustlings and creaks. She told herself it was only the house settling, until a squeak directly in front of her assured her she was not alone. She continued resolutely forward and whatever it was scuttled away into the darkness.

By her reckoning, she was crossing behind the grand staircase when an even worse sound assailed her. A gurgling moaning came from overhead, rising and falling. It sent a shudder through her and gooseflesh pimpled her arms. Could Brentfield be haunted? She had a vision of a hideous ghost dropping from the ceiling to confront her—The Banshee of Ancient Eire. Just when she would have faltered, she heard a muffled "Keep it down in there!" and the sound shut off with a swallowed curse. She had been passing under a snoring servant! With a nervous laugh, she continued on.

As David had told her, the descending stair led her to his bedchamber. She paused to wonder whether it was appropriate to just appear, and decided to knock. Asheram opened the panel and let her in.

Her first sight of David wrung a cry from her. He lay on his back in the center of a great box bed, so pale and still that for a moment she thought he had indeed passed on. Then she saw the steady rise and fall of the emerald satin comforter, ever so slight, and knew he was still alive. She took a deep breath and let it out slowly.

"He hasn't stirred," Asheram explained, leading her to an armchair beside the bed. "I won't leave you for long. I just need a few moments to close my eyes." He shrugged his shoulders as if to loosen cramped muscles. "It's times like these when I realize I'm not as young as I used to be. Are you sure you'll be all right?"

"I'll be fine. What should I do to help?" Hannah asked, unable to take her eyes off David. The scrape down the side of his face was puffy and raw, but at least it was scabbing. His long thick lashes fanned his ashen cheeks. Someone had removed his clothing and put him in a white lawn nightshirt with an open neck. It made him look all the more pale and vulnerable.

"Just stay with him," Asheram told her. "You don't even have to stoke the fire. Dr. Praxton thought the room might be too close, so we'll let the fire burn down. Send Weimers for me if David awakens." He paused, and she could feel him watching her. "You should know that Dr. Praxton says there may be some damage to his mind."

"D-d-damage?" Hannah faltered, facing him. "What kind of damage?"

Asheram's face was sad. "He may not remember the accident. He may not remember us. He may not even know himself. In extreme cases, Dr. Praxton tells me, the victim becomes like a little child."

"But it's momentary?" Hannah could hear the pleading tone in her voice. "He'll get over it?"

"Perhaps, perhaps not. He's young and strong, Miss Alexander. Most likely he'll be fine. It's simply best to be prepared." He eyed David for a moment, and a slow smile spread over his face. "There's not much that will keep this one down. Did he tell you we met on the boat over from America?"

"Yes. And he said you were descended from the King of Ethiopia." She hoped she did not sound skeptical.

He chuckled. "A family legend. We are English through and through. There has been an Asheram tutoring members of Parliament since the first Parliament was formed. We teach them how to walk and how to talk, how to display a gentlemanly bearing, how to win a debate. My last client, the Duke of Kent, was sufficiently grateful for my services that I was able to retire and tour the world as I'd always dreamed. I have friends on every continent, in shockingly high places." He chuckled again. "Imagine my surprise when on a trip home from America, the captain asked me to give up my place to a solicitor from London who was fetching the new Earl of Brentfield home. Of course I refused. Bumptious fellow. But the new earl intrigued me. He was so different from the gentlemen I had tutored. I found it rather discomposing, and rather refreshing."

"And now David is your client," she concluded.

"Oh, no, Miss Alexander," he corrected her. "David is not my client. David is my friend. I'm staying on only long enough to see him get acclimated. He'll make a marvelous earl." He winked at Hannah. "But don't tell him I admitted that. Take good care of him, my dear. I'll return shortly."

She nodded, and the door closed as she took her seat at the bedside.

She watched him in silence for a time. Her fingers twitched in her lap, and she wished she'd brought her sketchbook. His face was so serene, his lips slightly open as if he were about to speak. His dark hair curled damply about his face. Now would have been a perfect time to capture him; she doubted she'd ever get him to sit still otherwise. Yet she felt something was wrong. It was the same something that was wrong in her current drawing— his smile.

The need to pray tugged at her again. Her grandfather had always insisted that nothing was accomplished without prayer. He had also insisted that King James had misinterpreted a portion of the Bible. "I don't care what he says about charity," the old man had told her once when he had visited. "I've read the Greek. First Corinthians 13:13 should read, 'There are but three things that last—faith, hope, and love. And the greatest of these is love.' "

She wondered for a moment why she had remembered that now. Certainly she was finding it difficult to have faith in David's recovery. She wasn't very hopeful about the future with him either. Then she realized that it was the final issue, the most important thing, that was the crux of the problem—she was afraid to rely on love.

The realization stunned her. She had always considered herself a loving person. But the more she thought about it, the more the idea seemed plausible. Perhaps it had started as early as her father's death. She remembered feeling so lost for a time afterward, fending off kindnesses from her mother, grandfather, and friends. Her isolation had only continued when her mother and grandfather had been unable to understand her passion for her work. Teaching at the Barnsley School had further alienated her from those around her as she struggled with how to work with her students. Yet she saw with clarity that if she had simply reached out in love, she might have overcome all those difficulties.

In fact, when she had reached out to the girls in love and understanding, they had responded more positively than she had ever imagined. After today, she could honestly say that they seemed to actually respect her. And she no longer dreaded having to be alone with them. In fact, the idea of having children of her own was no longer so troubling. She might not be the best disciplinarian, she might not have the answers to all their questions, but she could love them.

And then there was David. She had been afraid to be his countess, but even that might be overcome if she were willing to give herself over to her love for him. What did that passage her grandfather was so fond of say about love? "Beareth all things, believeth all things, hopeth all things, endureth all things." Surely if she let love triumph, she and David could find a way after all.

Watching him now, she felt the courage to try one last prayer. "Please, God," she murmured, clasping her hands tightly together. "Give me another chance to show that I can love. Let David live so I can tell him how much I love him."

In the bed, David stirred. Hannah caught her breath.

"David?" she ventured. "David, can you hear me?"

His hand moved up to grip the edge of the covers, and he moaned.

Hannah rose to her feet, feeling hope flood through her. "David? Oh, please, David! If you can hear me, wake up."

He tossed onto his side, and his face contorted in pain. Alarmed, she bent over him. His breath came in ragged gasps as if he'd just run a race.

"Hannah!" he cried out, and curled tighter as if the effort hurt.

"I'm here!" she assured him. "I'm right here. Please, David, come back to me. I need you."

He stiffened, his eyes squeezing in a grimace, and moaned again. "Hannah, don't go! I love you!"

She choked back a sob, catching up his hand. It was hot in her grip, and she feared for him. Was she too late after all? "I'm here. I haven't gone. I'll never go. I love you too. Wake up and let me show you."

Her touch seemed to quiet him. He relaxed against the pillow, although his lips moved. Bending low, she strained to hear the words.

"What do you think you're doing?" Lady Brentfield demanded from the door.

Hannah straightened, clinging to David's hand. She had been so intent on him she had not heard the door open or close. That Lady Brentfield had entered so easily only confirmed Hannah's fears about the servants.

Lady Brentfield stood in her wrapper, a pink silky affair with lace encrusting the hem, long sleeves, and a deep bodice. Her golden hair was unbound and cascading past her shoulders. She should have looked soft and feminine. The anger in her eyes made her look lethal to Hannah.

"I am not accustomed to repeating myself," Lady Brentfield snarled. "You have no business in this room, not when you caused his injuries."

Hannah knew exactly who was to blame for David's condition, but she could not confront the woman while David

lay at her mercy. "I'm merely watching his lordship while
Mr. Asheram takes a short nap."

"Do you think I believe that?" The woman laughed,
moving closer to the bed. Hannah released David's hand
to intercept her. Lady Brentfield glared.

"You are here to get yourself compromised," she accused Hannah. "Admit it! You know he will never marry
you any other way."

A hot retort sprang to Hannah's tongue, but she swallowed it down. "You may think what you like, Lady Brentfield. I am merely doing my duty."

"Your duty," she sneered. "That's your excuse for getting your own way, isn't it? Well, it stops right now. I am
the mistress of Brentfield, not that black-skinned prig, not
that weakling in the bed. I rule here. Go back to your
room and pack your things. I want you out of this house
by dawn."

Hannah stiffened, but she knew she could not give in.
"No, Lady Brentfield. I am staying until David dismisses
me. You are the one who will leave this room. Go now,
or I'll scream."

"Scream?" Lady Brentfield laughed. "You wouldn't
dare. I'm a witness to your pathetic attempt to get yourself
a titled husband. You scream, and I'll tell them all what
you tried to do. Your reputation will be in tatters. Miss
Martingale will never take you back."

"You have until the count of three," Hannah replied,
holding on to her fragile faith for strength. "One . . ."

"You're bluffing. You cannot win with the hand you
have been dealt."

"Two . . ."

"I warn you, you are only hurting your own reputation."

"Three . . ."

Lady Brentfield crossed her arms over her chest and
dared her.

Hannah screamed.

The door burst open, and the young footman dashed in, only to skid to a stop as he beheld the tableau. "Lady Brentfield, what . . . Miss Alexander, what are you doing here?"

"Lady Brentfield," Hannah told him, "needs to see Mr. Asheram. She would like to lodge a complaint about my services. I suggest you escort her on her way."

"This woman," Lady Brentfield countered, "is attempting to seduce his lordship. I insist you remove her at once."

The young man licked his lips, glancing nervously between the two determined women and the still figure on the bed. "Mr. Haversham never mentioned anything about your being here, Miss Alexander."

"He asked me personally," Hannah assured him, head high. Her heart began to pound loudly, and she took a deep breath to calm herself. "I will not leave this room unless he orders me to."

The footman swallowed and turned his gaze to Lady Brentfield. "Your ladyship?" he asked hopefully.

"Oh, don't be an ass," Lady Brentfield snapped, throwing up her hands. "Return to your post. I'll find Haversham myself." She stomped from the room. With a puzzled look at Hannah, the footman closed the door once more.

The sound of slow, quiet, clapping came from the bed. Hannah whirled.

"Well done, my dear," David said with a grin.

Twenty-two

Hannah dashed across the space, and for a moment David thought she would throw herself into his arms. Part of him was decidedly pleased about the prospect, but his throbbing head quailed. She stopped at his side, however, and gazed down at him so adoringly that he felt himself blushing.

"Oh, David," she cried, dark eyes luminous. "You're awake. Do you know me?"

She was so serious that he couldn't resist teasing her. "Do I know you? Let me see. Cleopatra? No, Joan of Arc? Wait, wait, I have it—Aphrodite, Goddess of Love?"

She stuck out her tongue at him. He laughed, then grimaced as his head protested. She immediately turned solicitous.

"Are you all right? Does it hurt much?"

"I feel like someone's trying to carve a pattern on the inside of my head," he told her truthfully. "And they're not very good at it. How long have I been out?"

She glanced at the clock on the mantel. "Nearly fourteen hours."

"Don't go by that. I let it run down the first time I heard it strike midnight. It's enough to wake the dead."

"Then we should have wound it hours ago," she quipped. Suddenly her lips started to tremble. "Oh, David, we were so worried!"

"So worried, in fact, that you took on the bully of the county in a bare-knuckles brawl. You stood her down, Hannah. I'm proud of you."

She blushed. "I had to. I couldn't let her finish what she had begun. She's been trying to kill you, David."

"You've been talking with Asheram." He sighed, wishing the man hadn't worried her. "You have to see that the idea is ridiculous."

"Lady Emily doesn't think so," Hannah countered. "And neither does Ariadne and Daphne. Even Priscilla's convinced of her aunt's guilt."

David tried to frown, and gave it up as too painful. "But why?" He listened as she outlined their suspicions. Though the pain in his head made thinking difficult, he realized with dawning horror that the idea had merit. When Hannah finished, he reached out a hand and pulled her to sit beside him.

"Do you understand what you just did?" he demanded. Now that he realized it, it nearly unnerved him. "That's a woman capable of murder and you faced her down alone. Don't ever scare me like that again!"

"I had to do it," she replied, obviously stung by his censure. "Do you really think I'd leave you alone, at her mercy? Am I such a coward?"

He felt his mouth quirking into a grin. "No indeed, Miss Alexander. You are no coward. I am very grateful." The grin faded as he thought again of the danger she had been in. If he had remained unconscious, Sylvia might have killed them both and called it a lovers' quarrel. He blamed himself. Asheram had tried to warn him, and he had laughed it off. His cocksure attitude had put Hannah in danger. In fact, his entire outlook on the estate had put them both in danger. Asheram kept telling him he had to take things more seriously. Perhaps it was time he actually started acting like the Earl of Brentfield. He tightened his grip on her hand.

To his surprise, she hung her head. "You're wrong. I am

a coward, David. I told you I loved you but I was afraid to act on that love. I was wrong. If you still want to marry me . . ."

"*If?*" He laughed, then sobered as his head protested. "Hannah, there is no 'if' as far as I'm concerned. I want you with me. I can't imagine life without you. The only 'if' is whether you want to marry me. I have to remain an earl, worse luck. Can you be a countess?"

Her fingers fretted at the coverlet on his bed. "Perhaps not like most countesses. I couldn't ever bring myself to hunt, and I'm not sure I'd be much good helping you manage the estate."

"You just keep an eye on the art collection, and that will be enough," he told her, hope rising. He was almost afraid to ask her about the other reservation she had mentioned, but he knew they needed to reach an understanding. "And Hannah, about children . . ."

"I'll know what to look for in a nanny," she replied readily. "And I'll know how to love them. I'm learning that that's what really matters."

"Then that's a yes? You'll marry me?" He felt himself tense and the pain in his head tightened like a vise.

She raised her head and her gaze was so full of love that he caught his breath in wonder. "Oh, yes. God brought you back to me, and I'm not letting you go now!"

He found he didn't care what kind of pain was resounding inside his head. He drew her down into his embrace. Her lips were tender against his, warm, gentle. They spoke of a shared love, a future. He felt himself relax. She offered a quick caress and then she straightened.

"Where's Asheram?" he asked with a shakiness that had nothing to do with his injury.

"He's resting." Her response came out breathless as well. "He'll want to see you. I'll send the footman." She went outside to speak to the footman, then hurried back to David's side. "Can I get you anything? Water? Food? Laudanum?"

He started to shake his head, and the pain was so great the room darkened. He sucked in a breath. His anguish must have shown on his face for she cried out.

"David, what is it? Shall I send for Dr. Praxton?"

"Not a bad idea," he gritted out against the pounding. "And perhaps I will try some laudanum. After I talk with Ash."

She nodded, and he realized she was growing dim. Suddenly he was afraid. She had said God had brought him back. At the moment, he wasn't too sure. *Dear God,* he prayed, *please don't take me now, not when I've only just found her.* The pain intensified and he closed his eyes against it.

"David?" she ventured, and he could hear the echo of his fear in her voice.

"I'm all right," he lied. "Just tired. Talk to me, please? I wouldn't want to fall asleep before Asheram gets here."

She was quiet for a moment, as if she wasn't sure what to say to him. "You called out my name when you were unconscious. Do you remember?"

Trying to remember was difficult. "I was dreaming, I think. It was dark, and there was a light. I think I somehow thought you were in the light, and I knew I had to get to you. You were my lighthouse, my guide. I followed you back, Hannah."

"I'm so glad," she whispered, and he thought she might be crying. He didn't dare open his eyes yet.

"Now, it's nothing to be sad about," he told her. "I'm going to be fine, just fine. Tell me something else."

She was silent again and he heard her sniff back her tears. "I started drawing you," she confessed.

His eyes snapped open. She smiled tenderly at him. The pain abated.

"Did you now?" he mused, absurdly pleased by the idea. Then he remembered how her other drawings had seemed to capture the essence of her subjects, and he wondered what he'd see if he looked at his portrait.

"You'll need to pose later so I can finish it," she told him.

He grinned at her. "You mean like those nude models we discussed?"

The color flamed to her cheeks, and she stammered. He broke out laughing, and the pain stabbed him anew. As he closed his eyes again, he thought he heard the door open.

"What is it, Miss Alexander?" he heard Asheram ask, his voice drawing nearer. "Crosswell said you asked for me."

"He's awake," Hannah proclaimed, and David did not need to look at her to know how she felt. The joy and relief throbbed in her voice. He forced his eyes open.

"Good evening, my lord," Asheram greeted him.

"Good evening," he managed. "We have to talk, and quickly because my head is pounding. I believe what you said about her ladyship. First take Hannah back to her room and post Weimers outside her door. If you explain our suspicions, I think he can be trusted to protect her."

"I won't leave you!" she protested.

"And I won't leave you alone," Asheram added. "I thought you understood. Lady Brentfield is dangerous."

"Too dangerous to leave to chance," David replied. "I want her confined in her room and a guard posted outside."

"You have no proof," Asheram pointed out. "You cannot condemn her without it."

"It's my house, isn't it?" David countered. In truth, he hadn't expected such opposition from the two of them. Having to deal with it only sapped his strength further. But deal with it he must if he was to protect Hannah. "She's here on my sufferance. She can stay tonight but I want her out tomorrow. We can put her in that house at the foot of the drive until she finds a new home, preferably one out of this country."

"Do you really want Lady Brentfield out of your sight?" Asheram pressed. "She could easily hire assassins."

Hannah gasped, and David grimaced. He had wanted her safely in bed before discussing the details with Asheram. Now it was too late.

"Not if we cut off her funds," he explained impatiently. "Now will you get Hannah out of here?"

She stuck out her chin defiantly, but he could see the fear in her eyes. "I tell you, I won't go. Not while you're in danger."

"And I can't solve this problem while you're in danger," David argued. His frustration triggered the pain again, and he had no choice but to close his eyes and count off the seconds until it passed. When he opened his eyes again, Hannah and Asheram were regarding him solemnly.

"We sent the footman for Dr. Praxton," Asheram told him. "He'll be back shortly."

"Lie still," Hannah urged, bending to arrange the bed-clothes that he had dislodged. "I'm sorry I upset you. I'm just worried for you. Must I go?"

Her tone pleaded with him to let her stay. He had to remain firm. "I'll rest easier knowing you're safe. I'll see you in the morning."

She started to go, then whirled back to press a quick kiss against his mouth. His head screamed in protest; he smiled against the pain. As soon as she and Asheram were out of the door, he closed his eyes once again.

As long as he lay perfectly still, the pain lingered at the back of his head, bearable, but annoying. To counter it, he focused his thoughts on Hannah. She was in love with him. She had admitted it in the passageway, and her words and kiss just then had confirmed it. She had the strength to get past this fear of being his countess. Funny that she was so concerned about it. He certainly hadn't any idea how to be an earl; at least she had grown up around the aristocracy and had some idea of how to go

on. They would learn and grow together. He could hardly
wait until morning when he could see her again.

He realized he was starting to doze and opened his
eyes again. The room was in darkness. The fire must have
burned down. Hannah had taken her candle, and his
light, used so often in his passage explorations, must have
gone out. He decided to wait and let Asheram light it.

There was a movement in the darkness and suddenly
a heaviness smashed against his injured face. Bright pain
sparked across his mind. He struggled, pushing against
the formless weight that blocked his nose, filled his
mouth. His head exploded in pain and he felt himself
slipping down into the darkness once again. This time,
he wasn't sure that even Hannah could save him.

Twenty-three

When Sylvia had been forced out of David's bedchamber, she had stalked down the corridors, livid. How dare that insignificant strumpet defy her? She was nothing, no one! Sylvia should have thrown her out the day she arrived.

She had thought when she'd seen Haversham pass the dark sitting room where she'd waited that David was alone at last. The servants still obeyed her, if reluctantly. She had easily gotten entrée to the bedchamber, only to find that impossible woman barring her way.

There had to be some other way she could get to David. She had to act now, before Haversham returned. Once he was back on duty, she would have no chance to finish David off.

But how was she to get back into the room unseen? On her first visit, she had planned to smother David with a pillow and then tearfully claim she had watched him die in his sleep from his injuries. Now, if she returned, her visit would be remarked upon. What a shame she could not come and go as that art teacher did. How she had gotten to David's chambers without passing Sylvia's location, Sylvia could not guess.

Or perhaps she could. She paused in the west wing corridor. She had wondered whether the passage in David's room led all the way to Hannah's. Surely it must, and that was how the woman had reached him tonight. Sylvia had only to follow the same passage and her deed could be done.

The journey proved harder than she had expected. She found the passage easily enough. The silly woman had left the entrance in her chamber open. Sylvia could see the tunnel was dark. She lit the bedside lamp and took it with her. The way was close and clammy, but she paused only when she reached the crossroads.

The place was like a maze, a world within a world. She followed the path that seemed to parallel the main corridor. The beam was narrow. At times one of her feet slipped off and she stumbled. Each time she cursed and continued. Rustling noises scurried before her, but she refused to acknowledge them and she certainly didn't let them stop her.

The passage she followed ended in a stair like the one she had climbed. Light pooled at the bottom. The teacher had evidently left the exit door open as well. Sylvia blew out her own light and crept closer. She was already hearing voices in the room beyond. She reached the bottom and stood just inside the panel, hidden from those in the room.

"I want her confined in her room and a guard posted outside."

She grimaced. He was awake. Drat her luck! If he were sufficiently recovered, she would have a hard time smothering him. His voice seemed strong and insistent. She listened to make sure.

"You have no proof." It was Haversham talking now, and Sylvia nearly groaned aloud. Worse and worse! She could not reach him with his dog to guard him. She started to turn away.

"You cannot condemn her without it."

Sylvia paused. Condemn? Was he going to expose that slut of a chaperone? It was too much to hope for, but she had to know.

"It's my house, isn't it?" Was it wishful thinking or was David's voice weakening? She pressed herself closer to the opening. "She's here on my sufferance. She can stay tonight but I want her out tomorrow. We can put her in that house at the foot of the drive until she finds a new home, preferably one out of this country."

She knew he would tire of the woman! From the sound of it, the art teacher was so soiled David had no choice but to send his embarrassment out of the country. The silly woman simply wasn't fit to be a countess. She could hardly wait to see Miss Alexander's face when he had her packed off.

"Do you really want Lady Brentfield out of your sight?"

She froze. Lady Brentfield? They were speaking of her! Her entire body went cold.

"She could easily hire assassins."

So, they knew of her deeds. Dolts. It had certainly taken them long enough to catch on. They were even more stupid to think she would hire assassins. She certainly didn't want to be blackmailed out of her hard-earned riches. Still, if they knew of her deeds, she should flee through the passage and escape.

But if she ran away, what would she do for funds? She could not let them panic her into a rash action. They had no proof, she reasoned, or they would have had her arrested. Without proof, he could not cut her off. She was the widow of the former Earl of Brentfield. Society would demand that David see to her needs. He simply could not discard her without an outcry. He would have to keep paying her bills, and as long as she had access to Brentfield, she had a chance to find the art treasures, or get rid of him. All was not lost, as long as she had money.

"Not if we cut off her funds."

The words seemed to echo in the passage around her. She hardly noticed that the art teacher's voice had joined the conversation. Why did she keep forgetting that he was a barbarian? He had no knowledge of how things were done. The anger in his voice told her that he would follow through with what he had said, even if she protested, even if she had some of her highly placed ex-lovers protest. She had indeed lost everything, and there was nothing she could do about it. She would be a pauper, a nobody, as obscure and worthless as a Barnsley School teacher. There was nothing left for her.

At length she realized the room had been silent for some time. As if she were a statue come to life, she climbed through the panel opening into his bedchamber. David lay alone, eyes closed. Beside him lay a pillow. She moved silently to the bedside and put out the candle there. Then she slowly picked up the pillow and crushed it against his face.

Twenty-four

Hannah closed the door to her room with great reluctance against the apologetic smile of Weimers. He guarded her as closely as another footman would soon be guarding Lady Brentfield, though for altogether different reasons. She turned to her room with a sigh and saw that she'd left the panel to the passage open.

Thank God she had had the strength to follow that passage tonight. If she had not been in David's room, she did not like to think what Lady Brentfield might have done. She had much to be thankful for. David had been spared, and she would have a chance to redeem herself. His injury still worried her, but surely the fact that he was awake and had his memory was a good sign. Asheram had promised to fetch her if Dr. Praxton had anything but good news. She should sleep.

She moved to close the panel and froze. Voices drifted out of the passage.

"Where do you think it goes?" The excited voice could only be Daphne's.

"Probably to the attic, or some hermit's cell." The dire prognosis would have to be Lady Emily's.

"It's cold. We should go back for our wrappers before we catch the croup." That would be Ariadne.

"I cannot believe Aunt Sylvia never told me about

these," Priscilla complained. "This is far more fun than following the regular corridors."

"Girls!" Hannah called into the stairwell. "Come down at once."

There were muffled cries of consternation, but they obeyed her, appearing out of the darkness in little circles of candlelight, looking abashed or annoyed as was their wont. Hannah motioned them into her room. When they were safely inside, she closed the panel soundly.

"You had no business going in there without his lordship's permission," she scolded them. "Those passages can be dangerous if you don't know what you're doing."

"You knew about them!" Priscilla squealed.

"Well, I like that," Daphne grumbled. "It's our house party, and you have all the fun."

Hannah felt herself blushing. She took her candle and went to light the lamp by her bed. The lamp was missing. She supposed one of the girls had taken it for their exploring. She turned back to them, composing her face. "Fun has nothing to do with it. I promise I will tell you all about it in the morning. For now, you should be in bed."

"We couldn't sleep," Ariadne said with a sigh. "We were too worried about Lord Brentfield."

Hannah smiled at her. "That was sweet, my dear. He has awakened, and Dr. Praxton has been called. He's still in some pain, but his memory appears to be intact. We have every reason to expect he will recover fully."

They crowded around her, hugging her and exclaiming their delight. It took a few minutes, but Hannah finally managed to herd them toward the door.

"Now that you know, you should be able to sleep," she told them, although she doubted the truth of the words herself. "And would whichever one of you borrowed my bedside lamp please return it? I will need it to go to bed myself."

They exchanged baffled glances.

"None of us borrowed your lamp, Miss Alexander," Priscilla told her.

"It wasn't there when we came for you," Daphne volunteered. "I went to use it and couldn't find it."

Hannah frowned. She could not remember having moved it, but perhaps Clare had taken it during her tidying of the room. Still puzzled, she opened the door and ushered the girls out to the surprised Weimers. Glancing down the corridor, she saw Asheram and a footman coming out of Lady Brentfield's room. Suddenly, Hannah felt cold.

"Do you have her?" she called. The girls jumped, looking at her askance.

Asheram started as well. "No. She's not abed. What is it?"

"No time!" Hannah cried, her heart thudding in her ears. "Follow me!" She brushed past Weimers and ran for the east wing.

The dark passage had seemed endless, but somehow the lighted corridors of Brentfield seemed even longer. Hannah raised her skirts and pelted past the doorways and stairwells. A maid shrieked as Hannah flew by and Hannah did not apologize. She hoped Asheram and the footmen were close behind her, but she did not turn to look.

She dashed down the east wing corridor and threw open the door of David's bedchamber. The feeble light from the corridor disappeared a few feet into the room. The fire and the candle had gone out. The room was in darkness.

"David!" she cried into the void. She stumbled forward, hands outstretched, hoping she was traveling in a line toward the bed. "David, answer me!"

There was a muffled moan and a creak from the bed and fear pierced her heart. Her hands struck the footboard and she traced around it, stubbing her toe on the leg of the bed.

"David Tenant, if this is a joke, I will never forgive you! Now answer me!" Despite her best intentions, the last words came out as a sob.

Something brushed past her and instinctively she slapped it away. Her hand struck flesh. Someone gasped. The next minute Hannah was hit from behind to fall sprawling across the bed, David's body beneath her. She flung out an arm and felt a pillow go flying.

"Miss Alexander!" Daphne called from the doorway.

"David!" Asheram shouted right behind her. "Get a lamp, Weimers, quickly." Light flared.

Hannah struggled upright. David eyed her, panting. She knew her own chest was heaving just as rapidly. He quirked a smile.

"Thank you once again, my dear," he said, sucking in a breath as if it had never tasted so good. "You can fall on me anytime."

Hannah wasn't sure whether to sob her relief or laugh at his silliness. She climbed off the bed as Asheram and the footmen hurried into the room.

"What happened?" Asheram demanded.

"It was dark," David offered, "but unless I miss my guess, someone just tried to smother me to death."

"Lady Brentfield," Asheram muttered, while the girls paled and the footmen bristled.

Hannah found herself staring at the open door of the passage. "Someone was here. I think I hit her. She certainly hit me." She rubbed her shoulder. "She must have escaped into the passage."

"After her," Asheram commanded the footmen, waving toward the doorway.

"No." David grimaced as if the effort of talking was too much. "They might fall through, Ash. I'm the only one who knows those passages well."

Hannah swallowed. "No, I know them too."

"No," David said again, and this time he didn't flinch. "I won't permit it. Ash, you can't let her go in there."

Asheram was clearly torn. "Neither can we let her ladyship wander about the house alone."

"She can't go far," David reminded him. "We closed
all the entrances except . . ."

"The one in Miss Alexander's bedchamber," Asheram
finished. He nodded to the footmen, who pelted off down
the corridor once more. "The rest of you, stay here,"
Asheram ordered the girls and Hannah.

Hannah was most content to do exactly that. The girls,
however, crowded around the bed, exclaiming over the
excitement. David closed his eyes again, and she didn't
think he was all that tired. She herded them toward the
group of chairs by the fireplace and cautioned them to
lower their voices. Before she could return to David's side,
Dr. Praxton arrived. As he did not feel comfortable examining David with so avid an audience, she had no
choice but to usher the girls out into the corridor to wait.

"So, she really was guilty," Lady Emily declared. "I told
you all she was."

"Well, you needn't crow," Priscilla retorted. "What
kind of Season am I going to have now? My mother will
never come with me to London, and you can imagine
what the gossips will say about Aunt Sylvia. No one will
want to align themselves with our family. I'll die a shriv-
eled old maid!" Her voice had risen to a wail, and the
rest of the girls looked alarmed.

"Nonsense," Hannah told her sternly, although a part
of her wondered whether the jaded Londoners would not
react exactly the way Priscilla had described. "I'm sure
your mother will understand your need for a Season. And
no one can blame you for what happened."

The other girls chorused their agreement. Priscilla
looked only slightly mollified.

Dr. Praxton came out then to confirm that David was
out of danger, at least from the injury. "He still needs to
be watched for a day or so, and try to keep him in bed

until Easter, if you can. But I see no reason why he should not recover fully."

Relief flooded Hannah. The girls beamed at him. As they stood talking for a moment, Asheram hurried down the corridor.

"Ah, Dr. Praxton, I'd hoped I'd catch you. Would you come with me? There's been an accident."

Dr. Praxton rolled his eyes. "Another one? The members of this household certainly have a tendency to get hurt. First that strange accident with the former Lord Brentfield and his son, then his lordship, and now this. Who is it this time?"

"Lady Brentfield," Asheram intoned.

Priscilla started, and Hannah caught her arm.

"I would prefer," Asheram added, "that you all wait here. I'll come to you as soon as I can." He hurriedly led the doctor away.

Priscilla bit her lip, even as Hannah wondered whether the woman could have fallen through one of the passages. She shuddered to think of the kind of injuries that might result.

"Let's go join his lordship," Hannah suggested to the troubled girls.

They found David sitting up gingerly in bed. The covers had fallen to his waist and his nightshirt was open to his belly. The girls stared in fascination at the hairs on his chest, the flat plane of his stomach. Hannah found herself just as mesmerized. He caught them ogling him and pulled up the covers with a grin.

They chatted about nothing for some time, until Hannah could tell that David was tiring. He kept covering his mouth as he yawned, and his head seemed to be too heavy for his neck. She was glad when Asheram appeared in the doorway and motioned her out.

"Lady Brentfield has been taken away," he murmured in the corridor.

Hannah frowned. "Why? What happened?"

"She fell through the ceiling." When Hannah covered her mouth to keep back a cry of horror, he hurried on. "Luckily, she fell into one of the unused bedchambers and most of her body landed on a bed. She appears to have a broken leg and any number of scrapes and scratches. However, Dr. Praxton believes her mind has snapped. She smiles at everyone and talks about the ball her mother is planning for her coming out. He has put it down to depression following her husband's death. I think that would be the kindest thing to call it, for everyone's sake."

Remembering Priscilla's fears for her future, Hannah nodded. "Is there no hope for her, then?"

"Perhaps, but she will need someone to care for her constantly. Dr. Praxton fears she may injure herself. We are sending for Priscilla's parents. They will know what must be done."

Hannah nodded again. "She brought this on herself, but I don't like to think of anyone drifting away like that. What happens now? The girls and I should not stay on." Much as it hurt to admit that, she knew it to be true. They could hardly have a house party under the circumstances. The idea of returning to the Barnsley School was never less inviting. How could she leave David?

"Priscilla should stay until her parents arrive," Asheram told her. "But you're right that it would be easier if the other girls returned to the school."

And they could not return alone. She knew that. Her duty lay in getting them safely back to Miss Martingale. Hannah straightened. "We'll leave tomorrow, after the girls have gotten some sleep."

Asheram nodded. "I'll see that they get to their rooms. Perhaps you'd like a moment alone with David."

She offered him a smile in thanks. A moment later, and the girls had filed out with fond good nights. Hannah approached the bed.

David yawned, not bothering to cover it this time, and

motioned her to sit beside him. "Alone at last," he quipped.

She smiled at him, and when his look turned serious, she knew her feelings were showing on her face. There were so many things she longed to say to him, but she had to stick to her duty or she would never leave. "Asheram told you about Lady Brentfield?" she asked.

"Just a little. He's explaining it to the girls as he takes them to their rooms. Are you all right?"

"I'm fine," she lied. "Priscilla's parents are on their way. I'll be taking the other girls back to the Barnsley School tomorrow."

"You'll be what?" He frowned.

She sat straighter. "I must, David. I'm their chaperone."

He reached for her hand. "And you're my love. I need you more than they do."

His pouty look melted into one of tenderness. He brought her hand to his lips and kissed it. The gentle warmth seemed to fill Hannah. She pulled away before it could be her downfall. "But I have a responsibility to them. I'll return when I can."

"When you can? I'm not a patient man, Hannah. I want you to marry me. I need you to marry me. I don't want to have to travel all the way to another city to get you to do so."

She reached out and touched his cheek. "And I want to marry you. But the girls cannot stay on after what happened to Lady Brentfield."

"I don't see why not. I'm the earl, aren't I? If I say they can stay, they can."

She shook her head. "I think Asheram is right that it would be better for them to go. I cannot stay here alone without a chaperone, and I have a responsibility to the girls."

"You also have a responsibility to your betrothed. What if I have a relapse after you leave?"

"Don't say that!" she cried, afraid to even think it. "You're going to be fine. Dr. Praxton said so."

"Doctors have been known to be wrong," he argued. He leaned back against the pillow and narrowed his eyes. "In fact, I feel the pain returning now. You're growing dim. Hannah?" His head lolled to one side, eyes fluttering shut.

She knew he was teasing her. He had to be teasing her. "David Tenant, you cannot have your own way in everything," she told him sternly. He did not stir.

Fear seized her. "David?" she tried louder, bending over him. He grabbed her about the middle and pulled her down into his arms. She gave herself over to the joy of his kiss, feeling his arms tighten about her as his mouth warmed against hers. The sweet pressure raised an answering fire within her. When at last he let her go, she could not find the will to leave his side.

He smiled at her. "I take it back, Miss Alexander. You make a terrible chaperone. I'm afraid if you don't leave the room this minute, you are going to be thoroughly compromised."

Hannah returned his smile, her lips tingling along with the rest of her. "I told you, my lord, that you cannot have your way in everything. However, I think I can spare you a few more moments before I go tell the girls we're staying."

David pulled her back into his embrace.

Twenty-five

David did not wait until Easter Sunday before venturing out of bed. Hannah found him pulling on his tweed coat when she and the girls visited him the next morning.

"You get back in that bed this minute!" she commanded. Daphne rushed forward to prop him up as if she expected him to fall over as easily as she did. Ariadne stood by wringing her hands. Priscilla started laughing at them, and Lady Emily looked disgusted by the whole affair.

"I'm fine," David assured them, disentangling himself from Daphne's grip. The grimace as he did so told Hannah he was lying. "There are matters I must attend to."

"Now he decides to play the earl," Asheram complained from the doorway. "Much as I applaud your determination, my lord, I must protest. Dr. Praxton said you were not to rise before Easter."

"Dr. Praxton doesn't have a secret room waiting to be opened," David countered.

The girls were immediately excited. Over their demands for an explanation, Hannah raised her voice. "A secret room that has waited for who knows how long. It will still be there when you are better, my lord."

David walked slowly to her side and raised her hand to his lips. "What's this 'my lord'?" he murmured, tracing a line of kisses across her palm. Hannah felt weak at the knees but she recognized his strategy. She snatched back her hand.

"I told you yesterday," she murmured back fiercely, "you cannot have your way in everything."

His eyes twinkled. "Why not? It's worked so far."

"You're impossible!" she protested, feeling a laugh bubble up at the absurdity of the situation. She wondered whether she would always give in so easily to his smile and teasing. She found herself fervently wishing so.

Asheram cleared his throat and she found the girls regarding her with looks of wonder.

"Miss Alexander," David told them all, tucking her hand in his arm, "has agreed to be my bride."

She hadn't had the confidence to tell them the night before, not with all the more dismal news regarding Lady Brentfield, but she was gratified to find that they were all delighted. Amidst the well wishes, David somehow slipped from the room. She knew, however, exactly where to find him. After entrusting the girls to Asheram's care, she took up a candle and entered the passage again.

She found him waiting at the crossroads.

"Took you long enough," he said with a grin, leaning against a beam.

With a shake of her head, she followed him to the room.

She found the lock cut off and lying on the floor.

"I asked Ash to have this cut off this morning," David explained, kicking the debris aside with his booted foot. "But I told him no one was to enter until we did." He gazed at her. "Ready?"

Hannah nodded, mouth suddenly dry. David pulled on the latch and the door swung open. Both of them raised their candles.

Light streamed onto gold and silver and the rich hues of fine oil paintings. David ventured through the door, and finding a lamp on the inside wall, lit it. In the increased light, Hannah saw that the room had once been used as an opulent bedchamber. A huge four-poster bed dominated the center of the room, with a gilt-framed mirror as big as the bed over the top of it. The bed itself was littered with satin covers and pillows and bolsters, all in a lurid shade of crimson.

"And everyone thought he only enjoyed hunting," David murmured.

Hannah caught herself blushing at the love nest. But as her gaze moved beyond the bed, she found that the rest of the room was crowded with statues, masks, vases, paintings, and every other kind of art. She easily identified a painting by the Spanish master Greco and another by Rembrandt. David bent to retrieve a ruby pendant on a chain of wrought gold that must have belonged to a pirate, and draped it about her neck. "It appears we've found Lord Brentfield's treasures."

Hannah fingered the ruby, which was easily as large as her fist. "It would appear so. But we still don't have an answer. Did he know that Sylvia was stealing them? If so, why didn't he simply put a stop to it?"

"Perhaps this has an answer," David replied, retrieving a sealed note from the plane of the great bed. It was fine vellum and sealed with the crest of the Brentfields. He broke the seal and unfolded it. Hannah leaned over his arm to read along with him.

> *"To whom it may concern,"* read the note, in a curling masculine hand. *"I have grave misgivings regarding my stepmother, Sylvia, Lady Brentfield. I have spoken repeatedly and at great length with my father, but he refuses to listen, putting my suspicions down to annoyance that I must share his attention. Accordingly, I have done what I thought necessary to safeguard my inheritance from her cunning wiles. I can only thank God that Father never informed her of the secret passages that run throughout the house. I have hidden a number of pieces along them,*

as well as the majority in this room. If you have found
this, it most likely means she has done me in. Be warned."
Nathan, Viscount Hawkins, heir to Brentfield.

"So, it wasn't old Lord Brentfield after all," David
mused, setting the note back where he had found it.

"What a shame his father didn't listen," Hannah said
with a sigh, thinking of the lost lives from Sylvia's greed.

David caught up her hand and held it tight. "I almost
made the same mistake. If you hadn't convinced me . . ."

"If the girls hadn't convinced me," Hannah corrected
him, enjoying his touch. "We have a chance now, David.
We mustn't waste it."

"I promise you, I won't," he replied, bending to caress
her lips with a kiss.

By Easter Sunday, most of the area surrounding Brentfield knew of the earl's engagement. Servants will talk,
and their masters will listen. Hannah found herself thoroughly examined at services in the Wenwood Church.
Every time her eyes strayed from the altar, her gaze was
met by another woman. To her surprise and relief, most
looked quite pleased for her. When Reverend Wellfordhouse announced the banns for the first time, someone
started a cheer that was quickly hushed.

"He is risen!" Reverend Wellfordhouse greeted them
as they left services.

"He is risen indeed!" Hannah and the girls chorused.
As they moved toward the waiting carriage, Hannah felt
joy well up inside her. They were so lucky. None of them
had been seriously hurt by Lady Brentfield's machina-
tions. The artwork was being restored to its rightful
places, Priscilla's parents were due to arrive any day to
care for Lady Brentfield, and Hannah was engaged to
marry the most wonderful man in the world. She turned
back to see David teasing the good vicar until the young

pastor laughed along with him. Several of the older members of his congregation cast him dark glances, as if a minister had no right to so thoroughly enjoy himself. William quickly sobered. David grinned as he strolled toward the carriage to join them.

Before Hannah could ask him what had been so funny, Dr. Praxton intercepted him.

"How's the head?" the doctor demanded. "I wasn't sure you'd make it this morning."

"And miss all the ladies in their Easter best?" David countered. "I'd have to be far sicker than that. Look at my Hannah in her lilac. Small wonder everyone's cheering for her."

Hannah blushed at his prideful praise. She had borrowed Priscilla's dress for the occasion and the girls were in bright silks as well. Even Lady Emily had been persuaded to wear a sky blue gown that made her look her age, for once. Several of the village youths had noticed, but the girl had kept her head high as she walked past the admiring glances.

Dr. Praxton clucked, eyeing him. "You're still too pale. Get some rest this afternoon."

As he moved off to greet others, Hannah glanced at David. He winked at her and turned away before she could check to see if he did indeed look pale in his navy coat and tan breeches. She promised herself to give him a good scold when she got him alone, which would not be soon enough for her.

She was grateful that he had insisted the girls stay through Easter. Ariadne and Daphne's family had made other plans for the holiday, and Lady Emily's parents were in Vienna, so that Hannah and the girls would have had to spend the day at the school. Besides, there was no place she would rather be than with David.

The girls were quiet as they rode home in the Brentfield carriage. David could not resist teasing them.

"Doesn't Easter signal the start of this 'Season' I keep hearing about?" he asked Ariadne.

"Indeed," the girl responded, smoothing out imagined wrinkles in her jonquil-colored gown. "Mother is letting Daphne and me come out together, even though I'm a year younger."

"And how many hearts will you break when you're in London, Miss Courdebas?" he asked Daphne.

She blushed and elbowed her sister, who glared at her. "Not enough," she countered with a giggle.

David grinned at her. "And you, Lady Emily?"

Lady Emily eyed him as if she found him less than amusing. "I am already promised," she replied.

Priscilla stared at her, and Daphne and Ariadne were wide-eyed.

"You never told us!" Priscilla complained.

Lady Emily shrugged. "I saw no reason. It has been arranged since we were children. It isn't as if it were a love match."

Hannah sighed. The news was the one dark spot in her day. Now that she had found her love, she didn't like to hear of others being denied the pleasure. She glanced at David and saw by his tender smile that he was thinking the same thing.

"But you must have a Season," Priscilla protested. "Everyone will remark if you do not."

"You must dance at Almack's," Daphne murmured worshipfully.

"You must partake of the midnight suppers at all those balls," Ariadne said in raptured tones.

Lady Emily snorted. "Fine ones to talk. You don't even have a chaperone for the Season, now that Lady Brentfield is unavailable."

Priscilla sobered immediately, and Hannah opened her mouth to turn the conversation onto a happier subject.

"I have it!" Daphne proclaimed. "Miss Alexander can be our chaperone!"

Hannah stared at them in horror. "No! Absolutely not!"

"Oh, please, Miss Alexander?" Ariadne pleaded. "My mother doesn't have any social connections. We'll never meet anyone!"

"I don't have any social connections either," Hannah reminded them, gazing at David in appeal. He merely grinned at her and leaned back, crossing his arms over his chest. "I wouldn't even know how to advise you!" she insisted.

"But you'll be the Countess of Brentfield!" Priscilla protested. "You'll have entrée everywhere! I don't care what Aunt Sylvia said—a countess with a talent for painting and an earl who's a Yank will be all the rage! Everyone will want to meet you. It would be perfect!"

"It will be impossible!" Hannah maintained.

"It would be fun," David put in with a chuckle. "I've been waiting for Asheram to complete the paperwork for the confirmation of my title. I'll be called to London sooner or later for the king's approval. Besides, I understand I have a lot to learn about Society. Who could ask for more congenial teachers?"

The girls beamed at him. Hannah stared.

"David Tenant," she started.

He grinned at her. "We won't go right away, if that's what's worrying you. I plan a long, extended honeymoon."

Hannah blushed.

"But you can't wait too long, my lord," Daphne put in. "As you said, the Season starts right after Easter."

"I'll consider it," David replied, drawing Hannah across the coach to sit beside him. "But first, I have other things to tend to. Miss Alexander will be unavailable for some time. She has a dalliance to complete."

"And this time," Hannah added, smiling into his eyes, "the only danger will be in stopping too soon."

ABOUT THE AUTHOR

Regina Scott started writing novels in the third grade. Thankfully for literature as we know it, she didn't actually sell her first novel until she had learned a bit more about writing, such as vocabulary, sentence structure, and plot. After numerous short stories and articles in magazines and trade journals, she got serious about her novel writing. *The Unflappable Miss Fairchild* was her first novel to be published (March 1998). Additional Regency romances quickly followed (*The Twelve Days of Christmas* in December 1998, *The Bluestocking on His Knee* in May 1999, and *Catch of the Season* in November 1999). *Romantic Times,* the premier industry magazine, calls Regina Scott "a star on the rise," according to their review of *The Bluestocking on His Knee.* Her next book for Zebra Regency, *The Marquis' Kiss* (November 2000), is the third in the series about the marvelous Munroe women, with Genevieve and Allison's cousin Margaret matching wits with the Marquis DeGuis.

Regina Scott and her husband are the parents of two young boys. They reside in the Tri-Cities of southeast Washington State. Born and raised in the Seattle area, Regina Scott is a graduate of the University of Washington. She is a decent fencer; owns a historical, fantasy, and science-fiction costume collection that takes up over a third of her large closet; and works by day as a scientist at a major research company. She loves to hear from readers, and you may write to her at P.O. Box 7162, Kennewick, Washington, 99336-0616. Please include a stamped, self-addressed envelope if you would like a reply.

More Zebra Regency Romances

**LOVE STORIES YOU'LL NEVER FORGET . . .
IN ONE FABULOUSLY ROMANTIC NEW LINE**

BALLAD ROMANCES

Each month, four new historical series by both beloved and brand-new authors will begin or continue. These linked stories will introduce proud families, reveal ancient promises, and take us down the path to true love. In Ballad, the romance doesn't end with just one book . . .

COMING IN JULY
EVERYWHERE BOOKS ARE SOLD

The Wishing Well Trilogy:
CATHERINE'S WISH, by Joy Reed.
When a woman looks into the wishing well at Honeywell House, she sees the face of the man she will marry.

Titled Texans:
NOBILITY RANCH, by Cynthia Sterling
The three sons of an English earl come to Texas in the 1880s to find their fortunes . . . and lose their hearts.

Irish Blessing:
REILLY'S LAW, by Elizabeth Keys
For an Irish family of shipbuilders, an ancient gift allows them to "see" their perfect mate.

The Acadians:
EMILIE, by Cherie Claire
The daughters of an Acadian exile struggle for new lives in 18th-century Louisiana.

Put a Little Romance in Your Life With
Janelle Taylor

Celebrate Romance With Two of Today's Hottest Authors

Meagan McKinney

__In the Dark	$6.99US/$8.99CAN	0-8217-6341-5
__The Fortune Hunter	$6.50US/$8.00CAN	0-8217-6037-8
__Gentle from the Night	$5.99US/$7.50CAN	0-8217-5803-9
__A Man to Slay Dragons	$5.99US/$6.99CAN	0-8217-5345-2
__My Wicked Enchantress	$5.99US/$7.50CAN	0-8217-5661-3
__No Choice But Surrender	$5.99US/$7.50CAN	0-8217-5859-4

Meryl Sawyer

__Thunder Island	$6.99US/$8.99CAN	0-8217-6378-4
__Half Moon Bay	$6.50US/$8.00CAN	0-8217-6144-7
__The Hideaway	$5.99US/$7.50CAN	0-8217-5780-6
__Tempting Fate	$6.50US/$8.00CAN	0-8217-5858-6
__Unforgettable	$6.50US/$8.00CAN	0-8217-5564-1